THE ONE THAT COMES BEFORE
by Livia Llewellyn
ISBN: 978-88-99569-48-8
Copyright (Edition) ©2017 Independent Legions Publishing
Copyright (Text) ©Livia Llewellyn
All rights reserved
1° edition paperback May 2017
Editing: Jodi Renée Lester
Cover Art: George C. Cotronis

The One That Comes Before was originally published in *The Daughters of Inanna*, edited by Brian Keene for Thunderstorm Press, 2015

Livia Llewellyn

The One That Comes Before

DATE: 7:17 AM, FRIDAY, AUGUST 22, 2079
FROM: TMO
TO: +ALL AT NORTH SPUR M37; +ALL AT SOUTH SPUR M37; +ALL AT +EAST
SPUR M37; +ALL AT WEST SPUR M37
SUBJECT: EPOCH I END PLANS

SHE'S READY – EPOCH II IS ABOUT TO BEGIN!

ALL TEAM MEMBERS: PLEASE ASSEMBLE IN THE SUB-BASEMENTS OF YOUR
BUILDINGS TO GO OVER GAME PLANS AT NOON TODAY. MINISTRY OFFICES ON
EVERY FLOOR SHOULD BE CLEANED OUT AND ALL CONFIDENTIAL MATERIALS
DELIVERED TO YOUR FLOOR ADMINISTRATORS BY EOB TODAY, NO EXCEPTIONS.

FLOOR ADMINISTRATORS: YOU ARE TO REPORT BACK TO MINISTRY HEADQUARTERS
WITH ALL CONFIDENTIAL MATERIALS BY SATURDAY 8:00PM AT THE LATEST.

LEAD SUPERVISORS: EMAIL US ASAP WITH CONFIRMATION THAT YOUR TENANT
EMAILS HAVE BEEN APPROVED AND ARE READY TO SEND TO BUILDING
MANAGEMENT AT OUR GO-AHEAD; AND SEND US YOUR FINAL STATUS REPORTS ON
THE READINESS OF YOUR FLOORS. AND, PLEASE BE DILIGENT CHECKING/SCRUBBING
INDIVIDUAL COMPANY RESPONSES - YOU SHOULD KNOW BY NOW WHO YOUR
PROBLEM COMPANIES AND INDIVIDUALS ARE AND HOW TO HANDLE THEM. AS YOU
KNOW, IT IS ABSOLUTELY IMPERATIVE THAT ALL TENANTS AND THEIR EMPLOYEES
BE IN THE BUILDING ON MONDAY, AND THAT THEY BE LOADED INTO EACH FLOOR'S
ANCHOR ROOM BY NO LATER THAN 6:00PM - OUR KEYS' POWER IS DEPENDENT ON
THE FULL COMPLEMENT OF THEIR ENERGIES AND BIOMASSES, INCLUDING, OF
COURSE, YOUR OWN. YOUR TEAMS SHOULD USE ANY MEANS NECESSARY TO
COMPLETE THIS CRITICAL LAST PHASE OF EPOCH I, AND BE APPROPRIATELY
EQUIPPED FOR ALL CIRCUMSTANCES THAT ARISE. BECHER DISTRICT'S ENTIRE
RAISON D'ÊTRE DEPENDS ON IT, AND YOU.

THIS WILL BE OUR LAST TRANSMISSION TO YOU UNTIL TUESDAY MORNING. WE'VE
ALL BEEN TRAINING AND WORKING LONG AND HARD FOR THIS MOMENT, AND WE
HAVE THE GREATEST FAITH IN YOU. WE WILL SEE YOU ALL ON THE OTHER SIDE!

IN HER NAME,
THE MINISTRY OF OBSTETRICS
EL TORRES DEL PAIN
OBSIDIA

DATE: 7:25 AM, FRIDAY, AUGUST 22, 2079
FROM: DIOGENES.SEPÚLVEDA@MO.M37.COM
TO: TMO
SUBJECT: RE: EPOCH I END PLANS

DIOGENES SEPÚLVEDA REPLIED:
UNDERSTOOD. FYI, THE M37 TENANT EMAIL IS APPROVED AND READY TO SEND AS
SOON AS I HAVE THE GO-AHEAD. MY FLOOR ADMIN IS ON SCHEDULE TO DEPART
FOR HQ LATER THIS EVENING.

FYI, AS PREVIOUSLY DISCUSSED, DUE TO THE NATURE OF THEIR WORK, ALL 40TH
FLOOR LBA PRESS EMPLOYEES HAVE VARYING DEGREES OF IMMUNITY TO MAGIC,
BUT OUR ENGINEERS CONFIRMED THAT THIS WON'T AFFECT THE QUALITY OF THEIR
BIOMASS ADDITIONS - IT WILL, HOWEVER, MAKE IT MORE DIFFICULT TO MOVE
THEM, AS CONVENTIONAL MEANS WON'T WORK, AND THEY WILL THEREFORE BE
LESS SUSCEPTIBLE TO THE CHYMICAL TRANSITION AGENTS THAT ARE BEING USED
THROUGHOUT THE REST OF THE BUILDING. (ACTUALLY, WE STILL HAVE NO IDEA
HOW THEY MAY REACT.) HOWEVER, BY 1PM MONDAY, THE ENGINES IN THE SUB-
BASEMENT SHOULD BE FULLY OPERATIONAL, AND I WILL REPORT TO 40 WITH
PALGRANE TO FACILITATE GETTING THEM INTO THEIR ANCHOR ROOM BEFORE THE
DEADLINE.

ALSO, AS DISCUSSED, THERE'S BEEN NO DECISION YET ON THE PASSING, NON-
TRANS EMPLOYEE WORKING AT THE PRESS. NO MAGIC PROPERTIES - SHE CAN'T
CONDUCT OR TRANSMIT, THEREFORE HER BIOMASS MAY NOT WORK IN THE
ANCHOR ROOM. PRECAUTIONS WILL NOT WORK ON HER, SHE'S BASICALLY A
WALKING ELDER SIGN. ALSO: SEVERELY MENTALLY UNSTABLE. AFTER MANY YEARS
OF OBSERVATION, MY 40TH FLOOR ADMINISTRATOR (WHO, I'LL REMIND YOU, IS
THE REPLACEMENT FOR MY ORIGINAL 40TH, WHOM SHE TORTURED AND
DISMEMBERED) ADVISES THAT SHE BE DISPATCHED, BUT OF COURSE I NEED YOUR

7

APPROVAL FOR GO-AHEAD. PLEASE ADVISE ASAP.

DIOGENES SEPÚLVEDA
LEAD SUPERVISOR
MO BECHER PROJECT
ANCHORAGE NORTH SPUR, M37

DATE: 7:29 AM, FRIDAY, AUGUST 22, 2079
FROM: TMO
TO: DIOGENES.SEPÚLVEDA@MO.M37.COM
SUBJECT: RE: EPOCH I END PLANS

TMO REPLIED:
WE CAN'T TAKE ANY CHANCES WITH THAT FLOOR, IT'S TOO PROBLEMATIC. CLOSE IT OFF THE SECOND THE LAST EMPLOYEE ARRIVES, AND DON'T LET HER NEAR THE ANCHOR ROOM. KILL HER AND TOSS HER OUT A WINDOW.

DATE: 3:47 PM, SUNDAY, AUGUST 24, 2079
FROM: RUCAPILLÁN-TENANTS.ANNOUNCEMENTS
TO: +ALL AT BECHER.MERCHANTS.ASSOCIATION; +ALL AT CADWALADERANDPITTS.LLP; +ALL AT EICHMANN.FINANCIAL.SERVICES; +ALL AT FRANKANDFREISLER.ASSOCIATES; +ALL AT HULTH.&.COMPANY; +ALL AT LENKIEWICZ.BELANGER.APOSTOLICUM.PRESS; +ALL AT RIVERSIDE.CAFÉ; +ALL AT SUTAVARA.SURVEYERS; +ALL AT UI-TE-RANGIORA.SHIPPING; +ALL AT GYNEAS.NUEVO
SUBJECT: BUILDING HEAT ADVISORY FOR M37, MONDAY AUGUST 25

DUE TO COMPLICATIONS IN REPAIR WORK TO THE BASEMENT AND SUB-BASEMENTS AT M37, ANCHORAGE NORTH SPUR, AIR CONDITIONING WILL BE SHUT DOWN THIS AFTERNOON THROUGH MONDAY, AUGUST 25. MAINTENANCE CREWS WILL BE WORKING THROUGHOUT SUNDAY NIGHT TO ENSURE THAT THE SYSTEM WILL BE UP AND RUNNING BY NO LATER THAN TUESDAY MORNING.

THERE MAY ALSO BE INTERMITTENT POWER AND WATER OUTAGES THROUGHOUT THE DAY AS WE CONTINUE TO REPAIR DAMAGES FROM HEAVY SUB-BASEMENT FLOODING DUE TO THE RECENT RIVER SURGES, WHICH MEANS WATER TO KITCHENS AND BATHROOMS WILL BE TURNED OFF. HOWEVER, THE BUILDING WILL BE OPEN FOR REGULAR BUSINESS HOURS, AND YOUR WORK ATTENDANCE WILL REMAIN MANDATORY AS USUAL. WE APOLOGIZE FOR ANY INCONVENIENCE THIS CAUSES, AND WILL KEEP YOU APPRAISED OF ANY DEVELOPMENTS AS THEY OCCUR. WE REGRET THAT PORTABLE FANS WILL NOT BE AVAILABLE IN OUR MANAGEMENT OFFICES, SO FEEL FREE TO BRING YOUR OWN - BUILDING STAFF WILL BE WORKING EMERGENCY SCHEDULES, AND WILL THEREFORE NOT BE ABLE TO ACCOMMODATE SPECIAL REQUESTS. AS USUAL, WE ASK THAT YOU DO NOT OPEN YOUR OFFICE WINDOWS WITHOUT FIRST MAKING SURE YOUR THAUMATURGICAL/POLLUTION SAFETY FILTER SCREENS ARE PROPERLY INSTALLED.

EVEN THOUGH THESE ARE EXTENUATING CIRCUMSTANCES, BUILDING MANAGEMENT WILL OF COURSE NOT BE HELD LEGALLY ACCOUNTABLE FOR ACCIDENTAL DISMEMBERMENTS, TRANSFORMATIONS, AND/OR DEATHS.

RUCAPILLÁN REALITY TRUST TENANTS SERVICES

MONDAY, AUGUST 25

3:32 AM

Alex wakes up out of dead sleep, lets out a single gasp, and freezes.

She's sitting at the head of her bed: eyes wide open, hands clasped at her sweating chest with her reading glasses entwined in her fingers, feet tucked under her rear. Something woke her. Was she sitting in her sleep? She can't remember her head against the pillow before she passed out. She touches the handle of her beloved knife, always strapped to her left thigh, willing herself calm. To her left, the crooked window frame clutches a dying air conditioner in its maw, slow ticks and a trickle of cool air bleeding from it into the stuffy room—outside, the city drones its endless, mechanical night song. An unexhaled breath crouches in her throat. Something passed through the darkened bedroom—a dream or a sound—and tore the sleep away from her in its wake. Alex puts her glasses on and peers over at the lamp on her dresser. The small beaded chain clinks against the stand. Her tenement is in one of the oldest sections of the district, clogged with factories and smokestacks and machines that span entire blocks. Sometimes the distant flick of a single switch on a factory floor will rattle the rotting bones of the two-hundred-year-old building. Construction, too, sends small earthquakes through her apartment. Occasionally the couple downstairs fucks or fights or both, and the few pictures on her walls shake like chimes. None of these things happen now, though. Nothing indigenous or natural just occurred. She can't say how she knows, except that at this hour when she's usually asleep, she's never been so achingly awake.

The chain's swaying slows to a stop, and the air conditioner dies altogether into silence. Alex licks her lips carefully, as though something in the shadows might hear, and swallows. Her mouth tastes like shit. She's used to that. Last night, another night, just like all the other ones before: standing in the tiny kitchen in her underwear, fingers tapping her throat, pretending to stare at the cereal when, from the corner of her eye, the whiskey glowed like Rapunzel's golden plaits, the captive princess waiting for the black queen to release her from a tall glass cage. And then: hours on the couch, the soft clink of ice against crystal as pixelated television images washed over the room like a grey marine fog. *The last night,* she told herself last night as she has for every adult night of her life, as the hours bled out of the room and into the streets. *The last night I do this*. And then she tilted her head and opened her mouth, the nightly lie disappearing with the whiskey and her despair into the evening heat.

Outside, in the far-off distance, the whine of a motorcycle sounds out, breaking the spell. "Fuck," she says, to no one in particular, as realization steals across her that she has to pee, so much so that her muscles clutch and spasm in pain, so much so that she's once again surprised she didn't piss the sheets. Usually this is the moment in the night when she starts up, stumbles onto the floor and out into the small living room and into the even smaller bathroom, where she sits a bit too heavily on the toilet— none of this done with a single conscious thought, as her body knows the routine and guides itself, her mind barely acknowledging the nighttime journey, all done in a half- awake state, the better to collapse back into bed. Tonight— this morning—is different. She's too awake, too aware. Alex grunts slightly as she slides her tingling legs out to the floor, then stands, stretching as she runs her hands over her greasy face. It takes only two steps to her dresser, but when she puts her fingers around the lamp chain, she looks back at the window, hesitating. The blinds move slightly—the glass doesn't quite fit within the frame, and a small thread of outside air pushes its way into the room. She hesitates, then lowers her hand and walks into the next room. She doesn't want anyone to see the lights at her windows, to know she's here. No need to draw attention to whatever's awake and outside.

It's only four steps to the living room. The apartment is really nothing more than a single square partitioned into four: a bedroom, a smaller room that serves as her office, a combined kitchen/living room, and a miniscule bathroom with an oddly undersized tub. Her parents' living room, back at the old house just outside the ruins of La Noria, is larger than the entire unit. Still, Alex can't complain. The rent is affordable on her salary, there's enough space for all her books, and she still gets a selfish thrill whenever she tells people she has a real two-bedroom with original wood floors. The kitchen blinds are partially opened, and the light that sifts in through the slats, along with the shadows and the ghostly glow from the silent TV, now only a fixed station signal, makes the space seem larger. Using the light as a guide, Alex walks into the dark bathroom—as always, she leaves flushing for the morning, so the two floors below her won't wake to the sound of water rushing through the pipes in the thin plaster walls and retaliate with the obligatory wall pounding and shouting. She's learned to moderate her movements and behavior at all times, always aware that anyone and everyone in the building can hear everything, just as she can hear them. It may be her apartment, but how she lives in it belongs to everyone else, or so it often seems.

She turns the TV off before going back to bed, then checks the thermostat on the kitchen wall. Ninety-two degrees. She shouldn't have looked—knowing makes it worse, though she's not surprised at the number. The building is a poorly insulated heat trap and this is the ugly heart of summer. She can expect nights like this until the end of October, when within the space of a week, the apartment will turn into a freezer. When did the soft seasons of her youth become so unforgiving, so hard? A sharp gust of air lifts the kitchen blinds: with a metallic ping, they fall back against the screen. Alex tenses automatically, even though the sound is familiar. A year ago, a lone mouse made its home in the walls, driven up from the lower apartments by renovations. It had taken her a week to plug up all the cracks and holes—only to realize she'd trapped the mouse in the apartment. Two days and fifteen sticky traps later, she was the victor; and there hasn't been a problem since. Still, random sounds often startle her into thinking something else has found its way inside.

She walks past the half wall separating the living part of the room from the kitchen part, and stares at the cupboards, the oven, the refrigerator. The blinds ping again, halfheartedly. Everything sounds dejected in this heat. Alex turns, checking the three dish towels draped over the handle of the oven. Each one is exactly three inches apart from the other. Alex smiles as she touches each one, a gentle pat with her fingers that she hopes bestows some sense of peace and balance on the invisible mover. Every evening, no matter how bad it's been, she always remembers to slide the towels together. Every morning, she always finds that the towels have been moved apart, as if some quiet spirit has fixated on this particular task and no other. Ever since it started—a few weeks after she moved in—she's kept the TV on at night. Just in case she's not the only one in the apartment who gets lonely or bored. Yes, she's drunk and delusional, and there's nothing wonderful or wondrous in the world to believe in. Obsidia is a city in which magic is duty and currency, not wonder. But Alex lets herself believe in this one silly thing. Easier than believing in anything else.

The blinds ping again, several times in rapid succession, then grow limp. Alex slowly pulls the cord, the prickle of goose bumps spreading up her arms along with the thin plastic slats. What's outside feels like no sudden summer storm. The blades of the overhead fan slow into silence, and the usual sonorous song of all the district's machinery vanishes, as the distant steady roar of the rest of Obsidia takes its place. "Brownout," she whispers to no one. Beyond the windowpane, in the small valley of cobblestoned streets and squat brick buildings—the dusty nighttime slumberings of a usually bustling cluster of laboratories, factories, and their attendant warehouses—streetlights wink off, and all the delicate building lights follow suit. The only remaining electrical glow emanates at the far horizon's edge, a determinedly dirty orange that shows that the brownout is, as always, local only to her area. Becher—the aging district with the most machines and equipment per square block, and the least ability to use any large number of them at once without blowing out all the circuit boards. Sometimes, walking home at nightfall, Alex gets the impression that Becher District is simply one giant machine, a great engine comprised of billions of strange and otherworldly parts, with its tiny human and non-human engineers living in its midst, perpetually tinkering, fixing, improving, until the great moment its purpose is revealed and it springs into terrible life.

These are the ridiculous things she muses about at three in the morning. Smiling, Alex presses her nose against the mesh screen, her eyes quickly adjusting to the dark. All along the high brick factory walls, deep green and cobalt blue flames flicker behind rows of lead-lined glass panes, and faint rainbow trails of phosphorescence wind through alleys and across freight docks, their owners invisible to her mundane eyes. Occasionally something flows out of a doorway or up from a sewer grate, multi-limbed, multi-winged, languid and at one with the night. This is the side of the city she never sees, indecipherable and mysterious, a country seemingly a million miles away even as she crosses its borders every time she steps outside. There are people at her workplace, she sees them in the elevators and in the cafeteria, dark-eyed, magic-dabbling humans and hybrids who know these places, who visit them with impunity and ease. She wishes she had the courage to ask them to invite her in. She would learn their powers and rise over the district like a black empress of pain, reveling in every astonished, horrified scream. But she knows she doesn't possess even a fraction of the strange abilities that allow them passage into that shadow city. When she holds up her hands against the world, the only thing that happens is nothing. A discontented voyeur, staring from a safe distance, jealous and alone. A thaumaturgically disabled dreamer. That's who she is.

Three stories below, the trees in the miniscule courtyard let out long, rustling shudders. A sudden wind is rushing out of the heart of the district, like invisible tidal waters being pulled away from rust-clogged shores. The thick chains that lower the fire escape ladder sway and creak, then grow still. Alex feels it before she realizes what's happening—the unnatural absence of all sound, everywhere. There is never not sound in Obsidia. There is never peace and silence. And yet here it is; and it is horrifying. She touches the side of her slender refrigerator. The metal trembles under her touch. It's running, but she can't hear it.

A low, heavy boom sounds out—an explosion. She definitely heard that. Alex steps away from the window as she watches the bruised artificial glow of the city lights disappear below the horizon. It's like being punched in the chest. It can't be. Darkness rushes toward her building, gobbling up all the light in its path. This is the ocean of true darkness that is swallowing all before it, the great cosmic deep that has always been here, since long before the city grew strong enough to push it back. "No," she whimpers. There won't be enough time to find a flashlight or matches and candles. She grabs hold of the oven door handle as the lights go out all around her.

In the great dark, in absolute silence. Alex stands, shivering, hand painfully clasping the metal handle, squeezing harder and harder. There has to be something, some light, some mage's queer glare in the cobblestone streets outside. Stretching forward, she raises her hand to the window, to where it should be. Her fingers never reach the blinds. They find nothing, no refrigerator to her left, no kitchen counter to her right. Is this magic? Is this death? Images flood her mind, fruiting like overripe fungi: the building is gone, the world is gone, she is adrift, and the tiny square of aging timber her feet rest on drifts with her like scum on a pond of water, naked and vulnerable, a weightless blip on the back of the slumbering land. And something is swimming up from underneath the city, something is pushing and gnawing all the layers of the earth away...

Vertigo washes over her. Snatching her hand back, Alex loses her balance and her grip on the oven. She pitches wildly. Where is up, or down? No, she can't fall—what if she never stops? Alex grinds her bare heels and soles down against the century-old wood planks of floor, toes curled inward so that the nails scrape the wax. Yes, the planet is still below her, the building on its temperamental back. It must be. Her breath is in her throat again, as if the sound of her lungs expelling air will somehow disturb the vast silence outside—wherever outside is, if she's not there already. She feels like she's floating, and—

And the moment is swept away with the next rush of wind; and the leaves rustle and the lights flicker on, and Becher District once again fills up with all the little sounds and movements that keep primal night at bay. Alex finds herself in front of the window, staring out at the trees, at the quiet factory buildings with their crumbling faces and faded signs, the white warm human glow of electric streetlights banishing traces of that darker façade of the universe back into the shadows. To the north, the familiar aurora australis of Obsidia rises like forest fire, orange with flashes of other colors from other worlds. She steps back. The heel of her foot hits something soft: Alex whips around and looks down.

All three of the little dish towels are on the floor, intricately arranged in the sloping shape of a tower.

Alex realizes her hands are tight fists at her thighs, nails biting into the flesh so hard that half crescents of red appear when she uncurls her fingers and stares down at her palms. Without thinking, she takes two steps forward, knocking the dish towels over: and the refrigerator door is open, the bottle of beer is open, and cold amber liquid bites and leaps down her throat as she shudders in relief. It's just one beer, and she needs it. It won't affect her tomorrow morning—this morning—other than feeling a bit sluggish, maybe skipping breakfast for a larger lunch. On this, she's an expert. This is her magic. This is what she knows.

Condensation trickles down the brown glass. She runs the bottle over her neck and chest, rubbing the cold droplets against her skin, then tilts it again, letting the last of the liquid gush down her throat. All the while, her mind runs over the amount of beer left in the fridge (three bottles), the inches of whiskey left in the cupboard (five). Four nights until Friday's payday, and she barely has enough to cover tomorrow's weekly lunch with Ted. There's her bottle of work vodka, but that doesn't leave her file cabinet under any circumstance. She'll have to ration, or skip a night, unless she can sneak a couple of pesos or pounds from the petty cash box. No, too soon since the last time. She'll ration. The bottle clacks against the counter. She's done. Alex leans back, staring at the crumple of fabric in front of the stove, waiting to go numb, waiting for the booze and the too-late hour to work their magic and gently carry her back into blissful sleep.

"What was it?" Alex whispers the words as she stares at the front of the oven, at the crumpled towels. As usual, nothing happens to indicate anyone or thing has heard. "I ruined it." She stretches out a hand, not sure what she means by the gesture. "I'm so sorry. I don't know what you're trying to say. I don't know what you want me to do."

Her hand remains in the air, until it doesn't, until she finds herself shuffling back into the bedroom, her mind finally sliding into boozy sleep. Three beers means she has to skip a day, who can drink just one after a day of all this heat? Yeah, but if she goes to bed extra early on Monday, she can skip. That leaves the beer for Tuesday, and the whiskey for Wednesday and Thursday. And then lovely payday—Friday, and she'll be drowning in riches again. Growlers and bottles of princesses, all waiting for her to save them. She will.

Beyond the dark bedroom window, the waking city whispers, a reluctant and slow rumbling of flesh and machinery beginning their endless crawl into a not-yet-broken day. Her bathrobe sits in a crumpled pile at the end of the bed, a plaid flannel ziggurat. Pawing it into her hands, Alex slides onto the mattress, pulling the robe over her legs. As hot as it gets, she can't fall asleep without something covering her, a flimsy protection of sorts. Against what, she's never been able to say. She sighs into the pillow, eyes closed, mind already drifting with the hum of the fans. Beneath her body, the building lets out a loathsome shudder, as though picking up the distant vibrations of something indefatigable, unfathomable, leviathan, circling the lithosphere, working its way up.

Just the city, Alex tells herself, perfectly natural. But she's already dreaming, and her dream self knows the truth. Nothing natural at all.

8:54 AM

"Fuck, fuck, fuck, fuck, Mother Hydra fuck."

Morning light pours through the blinds, so bright and clear it almost feels like the apartment is falling into the sun. Sunglasses slipping down her forehead, Alex struggles with her jacket, trying to get the sleeve unknotted as she rams her arm through it. She'd forgotten to reset the alarm after the power went off, and now she's going to be late for work. It's always been a great source of pride that no matter how much she's had the night before, she's always been on time the next day, looking professional and calm. She's just a receptionist slash administrative assistant, interchangeable and replaceable, but she knows the editors and publishers note who comes in and when, and it looks better to be at her desk before ten, especially when her desk is the one everybody sees. Maybe pumped full of aspirin, maybe wearing a bit too much foundation to hide the dark circles, maybe keeping those sunglasses on for a bit too long: but early nonetheless. Being early even by a few minutes means she doesn't have a problem, or rather: the problem doesn't have her. Nope. This is one bitch who's got everything under control.

"God-shitting heat." Alex stares at the thermostat, beads

of sweat already forming under her arms and at the back of her neck. Already ninety-four degrees—unbearable at such an early hour in the morning. If she can't get the AC running again, she'll have to get a new one. Another couple hundred dollars she doesn't have, right down the drain. She never gets a break.

"Shoes. Brown shoes. Where's the fucking left one?" The telephone on the kitchen wall starts ringing. Alex lopes over and pulls the jack out of the wall. "I have no time for you bastards today," she mutters as the phone dies mid-ring. Collection companies. This has been a particularly bad year, and she's gotten a bit behind in payments, more than usual. Whatever, she'll deal with it tomorrow. It's too hot to think, to talk, to do anything except escape this misery for eight or nine hours to a cool, air-conditioned office. She's never wanted to go to work so badly in her life. One last swallow of orange juice, put the dirty glass in the fridge—she'll wash it when she gets home—strap the sleek commuter-grade air respirator onto her face, grab her little tote bag and her keys, and she's out of here.

Before she leaves the apartment, though, Alex stands in the open door, surveying her space in its tranquil entirety as if for the last time. As always, it strikes her how wonderful the apartment is, how small and perfect even with all its imperfections. Her beautiful rows of books, the small couch decorated with two expensive tapestry pillows she bought on impulse from Terra Firma Carpets in Market District years ago, the tanned leather masks she fashioned from the corpses of her ex-lovers and enemies, the buttery gleam of the century-old wood floors warming under the lash of the sun—this is the apartment she wants to come home to every day, even if when she does, she's usually too tired and too ready to drink to see it the way it is, the way she wants it to be. It's only in this quiet, perfect soap-bubble moment of the morning that she can appreciate all that she's fought for, see all that she's made for herself.

"I'll be back," she says, as always, and to no one in particular. To herself, the dust, to the quiet specter that moves the towels. "I'll be home tonight. As always. No matter what."

And then she closes and locks the door, and the dank hallway smelling of mold and seaweed greets her, and she navigates three impossibly narrow flights of carpeted, cobwebbed stairs leading to a lobby the size of a broom closet that houses six rusting boxes serving as make-shift mail drops, and then it's down crumbling concrete steps (the original steps having worn away half a century ago), and she stands on the cracked, weed-choked sidewalk outside the lopsided red tenement, completely surrounded by ten- and twenty-story factories and engines rotting and rusting away in the ninety-degree humidity of another pitiless August day. Alex sighs and adjusts the slipping bag at her shoulder, then starts up the street, the weird bounce of her chunky and unfashionably low-heeled walking shoes joining the other commuters as they trickle down the steps of other tenements, or up from cellars, or from wherever they hide in the wild night from their strange nocturnal neighbors. When the real estate boom began along the river's shores and new buildings sprang up like dandelions, forcing the well-heeled middle classes into the inner, archaic sections of Becher, she used to stare out the small diamond window in the front door, waiting until no one was on the sidewalk before emerging. She used to be so ashamed to be seen leaving the building, when all her new neighbors on the block lived in better buildings, had nicer clothes. Now she doesn't give a shit anymore, because she knows no one else cares. They're ashamed to be living here, too. They don't see her walking along the streets because they can't even stand to see themselves.

Down and around the corner, and across two traffic-clogged circuses to a seven-hundred-unit apartment building that appeared out of thin air four years ago—that's her first stop. Even though it's the opposite direction of work, Alex walks here every morning, even when she's late, to the little coffee house that appeared a year after the building opened. She pulls down her mask and sighs as she opens the door and crisp, chilly air washes over her. The line is horrendous, as usual, filled with the typical combination of office professionals, building residents still dressed in pajamas and robes, dark-eyed mages and thaumaturgists there to fill up on espresso and gossip before disappearing back into their labyrinths of spells and machinery. The tables are already filled, all the customers pecking away at portable typewriters or filling scale-lined notebook pages with the thick black scribbling of unsellable novels as they pick at their pastries. Alex loathes them all, even as she envies them, envies their arcane languages and exotic lab uniforms and the cool, wondrous lives they must live, filled with time and power enough to do and have everything, to lounge and play artists in cafes by day and play with the secrets of the city by night, while she's spending the prime of her life trapped in a cubicle, feeling her will to live bleed away.

And how must they see her, in return? A tall, large-eyed, thick-browed woman of ambiguous age and background, too light-skinned to be black, too dark to be white, with a big mess of curls perching on her head in a bun that looks like dirty cotton candy, sweating through her knock-off designer suit and blouse. Not ugly—dramatic is more the word. Probably some office file monkey, or maybe some sad-sack lab receptionist—but good for her that she's not working retail or restaurants, right? Of course, she's no size four like the more fashionable women are, but she's not a complete cow, so good on her for that, too. It's at this point, though, when their gaze moves up her body from her ass, that the wonder and doubt really start to race through their minds. The neat, albeit very expensively faked, silver bio-thauma port at the base of her throat that indicates she's undergoing constant mandatory thaumaturgical transformation, as all Obsidians must nowadays. They see how, in a certain angle of the light, hundreds of fine lines of plum-colored scars light up every inch of her bare face and neck, as though she was a living geode, her skin barely stretching across the universe of sparkling amethyst inside. But *of what specific nature of transformation*, of her obvious remaking, is the ghost of the question that sparks in lingering gazes that look for gills or horns or a ruby pineal eye, but see no visible physical or alchymical change, that see only the square and stony lines of her boringly human jaw. They see how normal she looks, and sneer and look away. If only they knew her secret power had nothing to do with their stupid magic at all...

Whatever. As a proud citizen of a megalopolis that is marrying itself to the greatest abomination in the known universe, there is no look of judgment or condemnation that is effective against her. She is the least strange and most mundane thing any of them have probably ever seen; but if they knew how many ways she dreamed of breaking each of their bodies open like cherry chocolate cordials and scattering their pretty insides across the artful pastry displays, they'd change their minds pretty fucking quick. Alex hands the barista her commuter mug and orders her usual—an iced coffee with a shot—and stands to the side after paying, watching the customers cock-block each other over the dwindling turbinado cubes as they talk just a little too loudly to their friends about nothing at all, as they ready themselves to spend the day doing nothing at all. Assholes. Losers. She'd give anything to be one of them.

And then it's back into the unforgiving daylight, back down the street and across the two circuses, which are now clogged with cars and trucks and even a few old horse-drawn wagons, to a small stop where she sometimes catches the red riverfront tram. She quickens her stride before jumping up into the back doorway as the tram slows ever so briefly before making a left. The conductor raises his hand and she nods in response. Every weekday she slips onto the morning tram, and in return, every week a fat package of romance novels and mysteries is delivered to his apartment, which he admitted to Alex he sells at a nearby bookstore when he and his wife are finished with them. It's a good arrangement for both of them, one of the few she has in life. If the desire to kill him ever arose in her, she would make it quick.

As usual there aren't any seats, so Alex stands to the side, one hand on a metal pole while she sips her coffee and tries to ignore the hot wind in her face as she enjoys the view. They're traveling down Avenida Anchorage, a wide, almost elegant tree-lined avenue that spans the entire length of the circular district, stretching in a straight west-to-east line from each of the circular river's inner shores, crowded with vast stretches of colossal office buildings and windowless warehouses. Like its equally massive north-to-south sister street, Anchorage shoots across the factory-clogged center section, where Alex lives. It's about ten after nine, and both ends are obscured in yellow haze; but the sun is at her back, her headache is gone, the air isn't yet so fetid that she has to put her mask back on, and the monkey trees and palms that struggle so hard to survive look somewhat less horrified with their situation than usual. Alex can't help but smile to herself. Even though it's a Monday, this is going to be a pretty good day.

For the next forty minutes, the tram comes to a shuddering stop at each ensuing intersection and circus, rocking back and forth as people get off and on. Emergency sirens wail continually in the distance. Usually they signal the start of large alchymical explosions or machine-generated quakes, but nothing seems to be happening yet, which unsettles her. Alex presses against the pole, refusing to give up her spot. Someone behind her places his hand flat against her back when the tram tilts sideways, and for a few wonderful moments, she dreams of all the ways she could bend and crack his fingers off, one by one. But her coffee disappears, and then so does her good mood. Never mind how late she's going to be—not even ten yet, and it's so fucking hot, she could die. *Mother Hydra, please make it rain*, she prays, biting down on the straw. Sweat wells up out of her skin at the back of her neck, trickles in sticky rivulets down her temples and waterfalls between her breasts. Every curve of her body weeps. In ten minutes, it'll feel like she pissed herself. *Please let it rain.* If it rains, the humidity breaks. Sometimes. Most of the time, anyway. Of course, the roof leaks, and water drips into her bathroom and the small bedroom office, but you don't get something for nothing, and she'd rather have a little water damage than another day of 115-degree heat. Anything to be able to breathe for a few hours, before it all builds up again. She sticks her head out the window like a dog as the tram lurches forward again, and sighs, both in relief and, as always, a bit of wonder.

Less than a mile ahead, Anchorage widens out, amassing

more lanes and a center strip of buildings as it rises up in a great graceful arch over the dangerous beginning and ending of Becher River, becoming Anchorage Spur North. The avenue crosses an elevated land bridge, straddling both the birth of the river—where it erupts from caverns deep in the earth and begins its tumultuous run in a perfect circle approximately the same circumference as London—and its even more violent end, where on the other side of the bridge it plummets in a mass of grey mist and thunder back into the earth, back to wherever it came from, or to some new underground country. There are no piers on this river, no midnight skinny-dipping excursions, no commerce or pleasure cruises. Anyone who attempts to sail it, who falls into it or jumps, is never seen again. No one knows how and when Becher River came to be, who created it and why, although there are constant rumors. Sometimes the mutilated bodies of decaying leviathans rush up out of the opening along with the black foaming waves; sometimes the waters are clogged with odd biomechanical parts, slick with oil or life fluids. Ships and train cars float through like broken egg shells, their steel sides gnawed on and clawed. What great subterranean industry or endeavor the river plays a part in, has never been revealed. Those in Obsidia who know have kept their secrets and served their masters as well as the Becher.

Alex stuffs her empty mug into her bag and slips her mask back on. This time, she also inserts the dense foam earplugs that hang at each side of the mask like feeding tentacles. Half the people on the tram are doing the same, as it begins its lurching ascent up the right side of the bridge, slowing down to a snail's pace as commuters drop off it like fleas. The humidity here is as unbearable as the constant din, almost unbreathable, and the masks help filter the moisture away. Other commuters begin removing their masks, small slits along the sides of their throats opening ever so slightly in the water-saturated air. Alex doesn't hate being fully human, but more and more in Obsidia, with every passing generation, it has its distinct disadvantages. Then again, those are the people who work in the buildings that line the outer edge of the bridge—in them or under them, repairing and shoring up the continual degradation that the water inflicts on the land. Alex slips off at the last stop, almost exactly halfway across the bridge, and crosses the street during a lull in traffic to the middle island, where a thick line of offices divides the right section of the avenue from the left. The thirty-seventh building, the last and the highest on the spur before it morphs from office park into a ten-lane toll highway to Obsidia, is where she's headed. Erected by Rucapillán, the corporation that owns all of the riverfront property, it's an impossibly ancient-looking, monstrous grey and silver ziggurat rising forty stories high. Someone once jokingly said it's been here since before the dinosaurs roamed the continent. Others whisper that it was brought up from the dreaming city. She half believes both stories.

Ten on the nose, her slender wristwatch says. Not bad for a late start. Alex reaches into her bag for her building ID. Her fingers touch something soft at the bottom. She pulls it out. "What the fuck?" She holds up a small dish towel, neatly folded into a rectangle.

The first dish towel. The warning. The one that always gets moved first, before the others.

For one brief, wild moment, she wants to run, run along the wide, crowded sidewalks, run across and over the bridge, run onto real land, into the real city, as far away from Becher District as possible, all the way up the city, up the entire length of the southern continent, up through the remains of the United States to the cold Arctic north, up and beyond into the dark of the sky, the dark of space, until the river is less than an eyelash-thin mote in the sun's bright eye. A hard wave of nausea washes over her, nausea and brittle terror as the buildings press down, the heat presses down, the air chokes and clogs in her throat, because every person born in Obsidia knows the precise moment when they will die, that's what they're all supposed to believe.

And she is going to die here, at the end of this day, in this building, on this bridge. She is going to die, broken and screaming and alone.

And it passes.

The moment is gone, and the workday has begun, and what a bunch of superstitious bullshit—now she's even later than before. Her paycheck on Friday. Her apartment, warm and silent in the day's golden glow. The vodka in her locked file drawer. These are things to live for, and she's going to live a long, long time. Alex shoves the towel back down into her bag, and lets herself be swallowed up in the endless slow spin of the revolving brass doors.

10:23 AM

Alex stares at her desk. At the mounds of manila envelopes waiting to be opened and rejected because the hopeful writers don't understand that Lenkiewicz Belanger Apostolicum Press isn't an actual publishing company. At the semi-sentient ivory-toothed typewriter, black and brooding at the corner of a rickety desk that is nothing more than a massive plank of shipwreck wood held up by rusting metal file cabinets. At the wall-to-ceiling glass doors of the elevator lobby, weeping with black rivulets of condensation and grime. At the hulking shoggoth-powered air conditioner that runs the length of the right wall, its pneumatic accordion tubes silent and still. She knew something was off the minute the sticky, vomit-warm air of the white marble lobby hit her face as she rolled through the revolving doors. M37 isn't one of those crumbling brick buildings on either side of the avenue. It's supposed to be the always modern, always perfect flagship of the North Spur where nothing ever breaks down. But now everything is breaking down—she barely made it off the last working elevator before the doors closed and she heard it plummet back down into the lobby. It feels like the entire building is sinking, and dragging them all with it into the bottomless silt of the Becher.

And another unsettling mystery—as she shrugs and wiggles her way out of her damp jacket, Alex notices something off-kilter about the door of the Ministry of Information-issued, refrigerator-sized safe just behind her desk. Leaving her jacket hanging like seaweed on the back of her chair, she steps over and grabs the thick brass handle. The door is heavy as fuck, but it swings open to empty shelves.

"What the hell?"

A single bright-pink Post-It is stuck to the middle shelf—has she been pink-slipped, with an actual pink slip of paper?

It would be just like Quartus, the single member of their Personnel & Payroll Department. Alex plucks it off and reads his neat handwriting.

ALL DELIVERIES

HAVE BEEN COMPLETED

BY THE MINISTRY

EXCEPT ONE

~WE HAVE FAITH IN YOU~

A cold little spark of anxiety explodes in her heart. The safe is where each night she deposits the editors' finished copies of ultra-rare grimoires and scrolls, each one hand-duplicated down to the very last archaic inkblot, insect part, demon print, and blood spatter by both magic and their well-trained hands. It's Alex's job to collect the books, to lock the safe at night, and to send them out every morning to select bio-thaumaturgical scientists and mages throughout the continent while Felix Pitts, LBA's lone editorial assistant, messengers the originals back to the addressless, ultra-secret Ministry Library in the heart of Obsidia. Last Friday afternoon there were seventeen completed books ready to be packaged up. No one notified her that the Ministry would be stopping by. Did she miss their call? Did she do something wrong? What last delivery are they talking about—the safe is empty. And what the fuck does "we have faith in you" mean?

"I've never worked at a place where the receptionist was the last to arrive. It kind of looks unprofessional, you know."

Vecula Threadneedle hovers at the edges of the reception room, paper-cut thin, diamond-pierced gills rippling along the sides of her pale-green throat. Vecula holds her usual eggshell porcelain cup of organic white seaweed tea, a rare blend her father, the billionaire owner of some massive shipping corporation, harvests and sends up yearly from private plantations deep in the Southern Ocean. Vecula's a typical trust fund creature—young, pretty, earnest, a truly dedicated and passionate lover of the intellectual mystique of the publishing world, who has never spent a single minute of her nine-month apprenticeship at LBA Press working on anything other than her escape from the gross pedestrian reality of it. Alex has been in the business for close to thirty years, and none of the boys and girls are any different or unique from Vecula. They come and go in windswept clouds of youthful dreams and ambitions, dispensing lofty and well-meaning advice to the full-time employees in the few moments each week that they emerge from feverish bouts of planning complex shopping trips in Marketside and extended vacations at their ancestral estancias located in the northernmost, pollution-free stretches of Obsidia.

"You've never worked?" Alex asks. "Is that what you said? Because, that I believe."

"The funny thing is, you didn't have to come in at all. Didn't you see the email? It's so stupid."

"What email? Why did you get one and not me?" Alex points to the safe. "Do you know about this? Am I being fired?"

Vecula looks more confused than usual. "What are you talking about? No one's being fired, although half of you should be. The building people sent out an email on Sunday, something about building repairs fucking everything up, but Quartus didn't send out his email telling us not to come in until half an hour ago. By then it was too late."

"What about the safe?"

"I have no idea what you're talking about."

"You said—" Alex pauses only slightly, not long enough for Vecula to notice, but long enough to imagine pushing the slender girl to the ground, sitting on her chest, and slowly sewing her bedazzled gills shut while giving her long cigarette kisses that leave a soft cloud of dry air in her land-modified deep ocean lungs. But her father is powerful and old—Vecula isn't like the other apprentices, with no families to wonder why their sons and daughters remained in Becher long after their apprenticeship ended and never returned home, so—

"—never mind."

Alex sits down and flips open a wide ink pad augmented with *Vampyroteuthis infernalis* mucus, specially created for the magically challenged office assistant. After pressing her hand against it for several seconds, she places her sticky palm against the warm computer screen and gently rubs. It seems like it takes forever for the grey snow drifting across the curved screen to dissipate, slowly revealing a small scroll of emails from late Friday and throughout the weekend. The usual spam offers for printing and paper services; cute rescue cat pictures from Marie, their copy editor; an updated publishing schedule and three requests from editorial to restock ink supplies in the work rooms; the email from Quartus; and an email from building management sent out on Sunday afternoon. Nothing from the Ministry saying they would be by to empty the safe.

"This is weird," Alex mutters. She glances over at the black answering machine. No flashing lights. "I don't understand."

"I have absolutely no idea what you're talking about."

"Never mind." Alex leans back in her chair. The air in the office is deathly hot, like breathing through layers of wool blankets. Even her apartment would be better than this. "Quartus usually calls ahead of time if the office is going to be closed. Did he try to call anyone? Did he call you?"

Vecula stares into her cup.

"I'm sorry, please remind me which apprentice is working for Quartus?"

"It was the weekend. I got a message, but I deleted it. I didn't think it was important."

"Yes, well. Come over here." Alex adjusts the small desk fan directly at her neck and breasts while Vecula slowly shuffles her bejeweled, sandal-clad feet across the worn rugs. She stops at the edge of Alex's desk, a look of determined stupidity locking her round eyes into place.

"Look at this." Alex rubs the tip of her index finger against a small pad of aubergine ink, then moves the arrow cursor over the email timestamp, almost hidden in the constant snow drifting across the cathode-ray tube screen that serves as a makeshift computer. Slowly the original time wells up from the faked early morning numbers, scrubbed away by her flesh and the prickly leviathan ink.

"Quartus sent this email on Sunday, at four p.m." Alex looks up at Vecula. "Something corrupted it, changed the date so we wouldn't get it until after we'd opened today."

Vecula shrugs and takes another sip of her tea. "I didn't do it."

"I know. You don't have that kind of power."

"That's not my fault. HR is boring. Quartus is so old, and he smells really bad, and he doesn't teach me any magic at all. I don't think he even knows how to. Honestly, I don't think any of you do. If my father owned this company—"

Alex stands up. Vecula takes a timid step backward.

"Yes, you are absolutely right. Everyone at LBA is a fucking moron who can't perform the simplest spell. Almost nothing works on us or for us, we're total freaks, and the most we can do is reproduce the spellwork of others. And *that's* why we work in publishing!"

Alex pauses, long enough that Vecula can feel the sharpness of it.

"Including you. Which is why your father dumped you here."

A slightly pink mortification washes over Vecula's seafoam scaled face. Alex smirks. If there's one kind of magic she does have, it's the ability to shut that bitch right up.

"EDITORIAL meeting in THIRTY minutes." Bartram Knapp, LBA's senior editor, stumbles out of one of the hallways, clutching the side of the wall and panting as if he can barely breathe.

"Bartram, are you—?" Alex stops mid-sentence. The dark wet patch running down his shirt isn't perspiration, as she first thought. It's vomit.

"In the CONFERENCE room. You too—" He snaps his fingers, over and over.

"I'm Vecula."

"VECULA." Bartram coughs heavily and runs a trembling hand across his mouth. Alex flinches and turns away, her stomach churning slightly. *If he vomits, I'm going to burn him alive.*

"YOU'RE taking notes. WHAT is with those GOD-FUCKING sirens?!" With a faltering push and a tortured groan, Bartram propels himself down the adjacent hallway, mumbling nonsensical obscenities at the bookshelves that linger in the dead air.

"He did not look well at all."

"He must mean you," Vecula states. "I don't do notes."

"I know you don't, dear. Everyone knows that."

"What do you mean by that?"

Alex lets out a whisper of a sigh as she shoves her tote bag into a lower desk drawer. They've all been told to be nice to Vecula, even if she never does a single useful thing—or any single thing at all. Apparently her father really is that powerful. "I mean everyone knows your talents lie elsewhere. You're far too important to be wasting your time taking notes."

A slight tremor reverberates throughout the building,

sending dust and fly wings off the shelves in feathery plumes. Alex freezes, her fingers gripping the top of the file drawer.

"Ugh. When are they going to finish?" Vecula mutters as she wanders off, a slender hand covering her teacup. "So annoying."

Overhead, the light fixtures rattle and sway. They've never done that before. The spurs are as solid as mountains, or they're supposed to be. Alex stares out the window. From her perch on the top floor of M37, across the thick mist of the Becher, the turrets, towers, and elevated railroads of Obsidia float in a gold-brown industrial haze, jagged and graceful outlines rising from the fog in all the shades of darkness one could imagine, as though the city is made of nothing more substantial than toxic mists and memories. She could be there right now, on the other side of the river. That little niggling thought still wafts about her brain, the thought that she should have just kept walking…

Alex lets out another sigh, long and loud this time, as she finishes closing the drawer. *Get your shit together, girl.* Automatically, she fishes a key out of the bottom of a cup of paper clips, and unlocks the bottom file drawer to the left of her. In a series of subconscious and well-practiced moves, she pops the top off her commuter mug, places it down in the drawer, grabs the bottle of vodka and unscrews the cap, pouring a good third of the bottle into the mug. She knows exactly how long the process takes, how her body must be positioned specifically so that no one passing through the numerous hallways that open into reception will see; and she knows exactly what to say and do if anyone does happen to linger and catch a glance. With the cap on again, she slides the bottle back onto its bed of cafeteria napkins, grabs the mug and a small bottle of Coca-Cola, her mixer of choice, and closes the drawer with her foot. Everyone at the press thinks she's a hopeless caffeine addict. They're not wrong. She loves caffeine, too.

10:56 AM

Alex never quite knows which way to go to get to Editorial's conference room—she just knows, like everyone else, if she wanders long enough she'll find it, almost as if the room moves into line of sight only and exactly when it knows it's needed. The entire floor that LBA occupies has been turned over the years into a vertigo-inducing layout of strangely angled hallways and odd rooms with extra walls that completely defy maps or directions. You open a door or head down a corridor never knowing quite where you'll end up. A long-departed art director once told her that the floor plan was a mechanical diagram of some sort, that he had figured out the design of the interior space, but not the purpose. He went a bit insane not too long after that, spending his last month of work doing nothing but sleeping in closets and slithering through the ceiling crawl spaces; and then late one evening, security found a portion of his head and half a leg in one of the emergency stairwells, resting on a pile of sopping wet blank legal pads, and an uneven number of fingers scattered across reception. The police never did admit that they couldn't find the rest of the body, although the massive stains all up and down the stairwell might have clued them in on the fact that there was little left to find. Then again, maybe those missing pieces were filed away for later use, the editors still love to say to the gullible apprentices, pointing to the glass cabinets and bookcases lining every available inch of hallway and office space, all crammed with boxes, caskets, phials, and jars filled with every arcane ingredient necessary to perfectly duplicate the grimoires and tomes the press is sent. Ground ivory bones, inky brown blood, spongy viscera that leave lovely feather marks against the pages, beautiful bright skeins of arteries and veins that unwind into cursive missives from the void. Soft, cured leather skin. Alex's mouth forms a wide, toothy smile around her straw. Her coworkers have so many gifts, so many talents. Despite her massive deficiency, she does have one gift of her own.

"What are you smiling about? It's a hundred and twenty fucking degrees of sweet moist hell in here." Felix Pitts sidles through a two-foot-wide closet door with several dusty books clutched to his chest and joins her in the narrow hallway.

"I was thinking of Federico."

"Oh good grief. That was hilarious. Bartram still bitches about the blood stains on the sofa, and it was almost ten years ago."

Alex deepens her voice. "Tell me, ALEX, what the GOD-FUCK does it say about us as a PROFESSIONAL press that we can DUPLICATE the most powerful books in the WORLD, but can't get HALF A QUART of blood out of a CUSHION?"

Felix laughed. "Well, to be fair, a lot of people have died on that sofa. We really should replace it."

"To be fair, I think those stains say exactly what they need to about our professionalism. It keeps the messenger service on their toes. Anyway, I'm the receptionist, the couch is in my room, and they're going to stay."

"You're the boss."

"Not really."

"Yeah, not really," Felix says, but his hand slips briefly onto her shoulder, surfacing then disappearing like a tiny kraken. "But, yeah, really."

Alex smiles and takes a deep draw from her straw. Felix is smart and witty and handsome, with bands of premature silver at his dark-haired temples that only make him look far more attractive to Alex than if he were younger. He's that type of man who's charming and complimentary to ugly women; and he's always been especially charming and complimentary to her, although in a slightly condescending way. He knows she's attracted to him, and he's just cruel enough to enjoy it and egg her on, because it amuses him to see what he believes is the delusional pining and pain of a sexless spinster. She's known him for almost twenty years now, ever since he moved from the watery ruins of the northeastern continent down to Becher, his graduate degree in arcane languages coiled in his lanky hands. Twenty years. Twenty years of longing to feel him inside of her, hot and hard, his tears dripping down onto her face as her hands follow her favorite knife through his chest, all that hot wet red blood coating her quaking flesh as he comes, and goes, in her arms. But she's spent her life longing for all kinds of things she can't have; and, unlike all those little apprentices, Felix would be missed, so.

So.

She takes another long drink from her mug.

They walk down the halls in comfortable silence now, concentrating on their desire to find the conference room, turning left and right along the creaking wood planks, swerving past mounds of yellowing papers that rustle in their wake. The floor is sepulchre-quiet, as usual: there are only eleven employees at the press, and Alex often goes weeks without running into any of them in the flesh, their presence known only by the crumpled notes Felix passes back and forth to each of them. Sometimes she wanders the halls for hours, tiptoeing and barely breathing, listening to the distant crack of the wings of birds or the scuttling of clawed creatures that have made their way through hidden holes, following the strange whispers of musical chanting from the editors' radios and gramophones, seeking elusive rays of strange light that stream in from star-shaped windows and out of half-hidden closets filled with glass jars of pale creatures that stir and shudder in amber fluids. She walks the empty hallways, telling herself she's just walking, just wandering, not looking for anything, but she's always looking, she knows exactly what she wants to find, exactly what she wants to do.

"Wait." Alex stops before a door. It's cracked slightly open, revealing a tantalizing glimpse of clean, empty space.

"What?" As usual, Felix steps back, letting her move forward. They all do, in situations like this. Even though they don't say it, they all know her ugly secret.

She pushes at the door, and it swings into a completely

cleaned-out office. The wood furniture has a soft sheen to it, as though it's never been used. Light bands of dust float over the empty shelves and a desktop barren of everything except a stained paper coffee cup and one slightly chewed pencil. Alex sniffs at the air. Cleaner, or maybe cologne.

"Nothing untoward," Alex says as she steps inside. "Just, I haven't seen an empty office here since—" She lets the sentence die, faster than the former art director.

"Did someone leave?"

"Not that I've heard. I mean, I guess I have no idea. I probably haven't seen half the rooms on this floor. You?"

"I've never seen this office before," Felix replies, as he begins sliding file drawers open and shut. "It's not Editorial or Production. No ink stains or burn marks on the desktop. The floor is spotless. Everything is too clean. It's like one of those furniture showrooms. All that's missing are the price tags."

Alex steps over to the window. A very thin stream of air moans and whistles through an invisible crack in the triangular frame. Behind her, she hears the hushed rustle of Felix's movements as he works his way through the room. Alex presses the tip of her nose against the burning hot glass. As her eyes adjust to the brilliant outside glare, that cold hard snowstorm of anxiety blossoms throughout her chest again.

"Felix. Take a look at this." She hears him walk up behind her, hears his low exhalation of breath.

From their vantage point on the fortieth and final floor of M37, Alex can watch the entire circular width and length of the district as if it's a silent film: the gleaming ring of fog from the river, the glint of rooftops and windows, the insect glisten of moving traffic. She can see all the way to Anchorage East, South, and West spurs, all crossing the roaring river like giant clamps locking a metallic disk of thaumaturgical movement firmly in place. From here, she notes how the avenues and streets circle, merge, and diverge like the massive cogs of some otherworldly mechanism, how the great factories and cyclopean engines lining the roads gyre and shudder in place, sending out oily columns of black and emerald smoke veined with ruby fire. A faint green shimmer, paler than the polluted gold of the air, coats every rooftop, rising up in puffs and coils from the vibrating ground. And all across the district, from one curved side of Becher to the other, hundreds of small aircraft crowd the skies. They hover at the rivers edges like insects, sometimes darting across the district and disappearing into the tangle of flywheels and pipe stacks. Others rise up from behind bulb-headed cooling towers and star-shaped office buildings, brightly colored shipping containers swaying below them in silver chain harnesses that they ferry through the mist, disappearing into Obsidia. Movement—above, everywhere. A prime swarm of bees, abandoning the old nest.

Every Obsidian knows the exact moment they will die.

"Wow!" Felix seems more impressed than concerned. Apparently he's going to be just fine today. "I thought Becher was a no-fly zone."

"Sometimes the factories get permission to fly equipment in, but I've never seen anything being flown out," Alex says. She calculates: it would take her at least two hours from here to walk to the Obsidia side of the spur. But with no money, no luggage, no family or friends, where would she have gone after that? It's all so obvious from up here. There has never been another place. "Something's going on." The words feel heavy and slow against her tongue. It's all that futility, coating them like slime. And anger—this is how she's going to spend the last hours of her life, in a fucking editorial meeting?

"Something's always going on." Felix moves over to the other window, pressing his face against the glass. "I've seen far weirder things here. Remember when they found that mile-wide trapdoor spider nest in the landfill?"

"Speaking of weird," Alex says as she watches a sleek multi-winged aircraft barely miss sheering the tops off a row of fat chimney stacks, "do you know anything about someone from the Ministry clearing out the safe in reception? I came in this morning and it was empty. There was just a note saying all deliveries had been made."

"No, no one told me anything about that."

"You haven't seen anyone from the Ministry here? It would have been Friday after closing, or early this morning."

"No." He draws the word out as though it's an entire sentence. Alex gives Felix a sharp glance. He's still staring out the window, his fingertips drawing circles in the light coating of dust on the sills.

"Felix, do you know something?"

"No, I don't know anything," he says. "It's just...Quartus had me hand over all the Library deliveries on Friday. He said he'd take care of them himself."

"But he's done that before, right?"

"I don't mean he'd mail them out, he's done that before." Felix turns, wiping his hands against his pants. "He said he'd be delivering them himself to the Library in person—he was summoned there this weekend. He left with them on Friday, right after work. So maybe he took your copies, too?"

"That doesn't make any sense. The copies go all over Obsidia, not back to the Library. There'd be no reason for him to take them, unless—"

"—unless he was told to bring them. When the Library

tells you to do something, you do it."

"Is he in today?"

"No," Felix said. "He said not to expect him today."

"Oh." She turns back to the window. She leans into the glass, letting her body rest against the wall. All the little tremors and quakes travel up from the earth, from the foundations of the building, pour into her body. Outside, aircraft stream up and away from Becher like ashes flaking off a burning corpse. Sirens, unending, faint and high.

"He took them because the press has finished its job, its—its—*raison d'être*. He took them because we're closed for business."

"That's ridiculous. Bartram would have told us. We would have gotten some kind of notice."

"We're getting our notice right fucking now, Felix—look outside." Alex reaches out to the desk for her mug, and a wave of dizziness hits her. What's happening is real: this is her last day of life. She clutches at the back of the wooden chair, willing herself steady.

"You're drunk," Felix says, moving away to the door. "Again."

She rolls her eyes, then grabs her mug. "Hardly. It's far too early in the day."

"You know, I always defended you. I've been covering your ass for twenty years."

"I know. It's kind of sad, actually, since the only thing making me nauseous for the past twenty—*thirty*—years has been working here." The shock on his face would be unbearable, except she feels that heaviness in her chest dissipating, rising up out of her as if she is Becher itself, and all the fears she should be feeling are being magically airlifted away. She smiles. "You really want to stop me from drinking? Because I have a little secret to tell you: it's the booze that keeps me from turning all of you inside out like human socks."

"Oh, yeah, evil Alex, receptionist and killing machine, who can barely do enough magic to change the toner in the copy machine. That's just sad. Sad and delusional."

"Fine. If you don't believe me, come to reception after work and sit on that couch for a while. See what happens."

"Ugh, fine, whatever," Felix says. He really doesn't believe her, she realizes. All he sees is a middle-aged joke. "When Quartus is back in the office, I'm filing a request for your termination. No one's going to be out of a job here except you. No more putting up with your ridiculous behavior. I have no idea why you're acting like this, but honestly? I'm glad, because I'm through making excuses for you."

"I'm going to die today," Alex says. "That's my excuse. How about you?"

"Is this what menopause does to women?"

"That's what I thought." Alex pushes her pad and pencil off the desk. They drop into the metal garbage can with a heavy clank. She sits down and swivels around in a slow circle until she faces the windows again. "Please tell Bartram I'm not taking any more fucking notes at his fucking useless meetings."

"So you quit?"

"No, I'll never quit." She sucks at her straw. The Coke is warm and flat, and she can barely detect the vodka. She'll need to remedy that, soon. "I'll never leave this place."

"Well, good luck with that." She hears Felix walk out into the hall. "Because Bartram is going to fire your ass right after I tell him, so yeah. Best of luck!" He shuts the door firmly—not quite a slam, but hard enough for her to get the point. She hears him shout *crazy bitch!* as he heads down the hallway, and then it's silent. That small creeping anxiety trickles into her chest again as she stares up into the cloudless sky. Somewhere, beyond all this magic and filth, there is a clean, clear, bright blue. She swivels around and places her arms and head against the desk, closing her eyes. It's stupid to take a nap right now, the world is coming down around her head even as it's rising up above her, she has so few hours left and she'll never see her little apartment again, so few hours until the late afternoon, when the night starts to bleed indigo up into all the corners of the city, and she'll see that sky, see that perfect clear blue, she'll be flying away from it, down and into the animate emerald abyss, screaming, screaming, screaming...

12:53 PM

She's standing at the kitchen window, watching the world burn outside in a hot-white roar while she waits for the cake to finish baking. It's not a cake she herself has baked—Alex can barely handle putting her takeaway leftovers in the sputtering icebox, even toasting bread in the morning is utterly beyond her capabilities or interest— but there's something in the oven that's bursting into hot angry life, and it's her job to see it through, because it's her kitchen. And that's what she does, she sees things through. Buildings crumble outside like soft sponge in the pyroclastic flames as she whips buttercream frosting into high stiff peaks with a steel whisk. And something beneath the surface is vibrating, throbbing and thrumming, sending waves of teeth-chattering energy up through her bones.

Something's coming, she whispers to the frosting, *and it's going to do to us what I'm doing to you.*

The soft ping of the bell on her kitchen timer sounds

out. It's done. She bends down toward the misted glass oven door, fear writhing throughout her as quickly as whatever it is that's moving on the rack inside—

Alex jerks her head up from the desk. How long has she been here? A stale, sticky film of sugar and alcohol coats her mouth and teeth. She leans back in the chair, running her tongue around her mouth and swallowing hard as she checks the tiny face of her wristwatch, although the strange new angle of the sun pouring through the windows tells her all she needs to know. The editorial meeting is probably long over, and so is Felix's meeting with Bartram, if he was true to his word. Then again, that's assuming Bartram didn't fire all of them already.

"Never mind. It doesn't matter," she mutters to the empty room. She wishes she fully believed what she was saying. If she doesn't actually die today, Alex and her bank account are going to be in a shitload of trouble tomorrow.

ping

Confusion and cold unease wash over her, driving her headache deep inside. Was that an elevator bell? But she's nowhere near the elevator banks, they're in the center of the building, and this office is at the far southern side. She rubs her eyes, then stops, cursing softly as she examines the smudges of mascara and eye shadow against her knuckles. Great, now she probably looks like a fucking ghoul. Alex glances out the window. The skies are largely empty now, only a few stragglers circling up and away. A small sigh leaks from her mouth, ragged and fluttery and weak like the beat of her heart.

ping

This time it's louder, and it's definitely an elevator, one of those slow-moving, old-fashioned water-powered cars that sounds out its aches and pain with every floor it passes; and it's definitely coming up to this room. Alex stands up and walks quietly over to the small closet door on her right. Felix had tried the handle earlier, but it was locked. She tries the handle again, then presses her ear and hands against the slightly vibrating wood. The entire building is vibrating steadily, she realizes. That wasn't just part of her dream. *Wait for it, wait*—and the ping again, loud and clear. And now all the buzz of sleep and the last vestiges of the booze burn away in a snap. It's not like she feels it stealing over her. This sensation of knowing that what she longs to do has become what she *will* do, because it's always there, this is who she really is, unmuted and uncaged from the conventions and social trappings of the world. She has nothing to lose.

ping

Quickly, her body flowing like mercury, Alex turns the chair to face the closet door, places her mug on the seat, grabs her pen, then presses herself flat against the wall just to the left of the door frame, right arm raised, muscles flexing in place. The pen is silver, long and sharp, and when she clicks the button at the top, the extra-long nib emerges like a stinger. Alex runs her tongue over all the smooth and sharp edges of her teeth. There's no magic to it. She doesn't need it. It's an ordinary ink pen with a nice little supply of tourmaline-colored ink with a dash of tranquilizer; and she's simply going to do a little cursive writing with it. Her left hand slides down her thigh, lifts her skirt, and unsheathes her knife. It too is vibrating, with a power and purpose all its own. Her knife is not ordinary at all.

ping

The sky outside has taken on a dark cast, sending queer shadows slithering through the windows and across the office walls. A deep rumbling rattles the windows and sends dust whirling through the air. A cnidarian airship, something massive and leviathan, genetically engineered to transport biologically dangerous machines in and out of the Southern Ocean relocation site. Probably a lion's mane transport. She'd seen once long ago, when she was a teenager and still in trade school, its bloated, tentacled mass blocking out the sun as it soared along the southern edges of Becher.

PING

Alex stares at the wall across the room, at the empty bookshelves, at the smeared dust lines where a picture used to hang from a rusting nail still sticking out of the cream plaster. She stares at the nail. There is nothing in the room but the nail, adamantine and alone. There is nothing in the world but the nail.

The nail.

The nail.

The nail.

The nail.

The nail.

PING

She hears a metal grate sliding open into the wall behind her, and then the closet door swings out. Silence. The knife hums in her hand, and the oscillation of the metal sends all the blood rushing between her legs. Whoever he is, Alex knows he's looking at the mug. He's moving forward—a hand emerges into view as he reaches out, followed by legs, a torso, and he stands before the mug, curious, picking it up. She darts forward, silent and swift, right behind him, and her arm swings up and back and slams hard into the side of his neck. Gurgling, little spurts and squirts of bright red blood. Later, when she's cleaned up, she'll use the blood from the pen to write up her weekend grocery list, Malbec and whiskey at the top, if there's enough cash in his wallet.

Alex's hand moves up under the edge of his fine wool jacket. This requires no effort—the knife guides the full weight of her body for her, and she merely follows, leaning in and thrusting up with all her might not because she has to but because she wants to, because they are a team, they are fucking this man to the death together. Alex grasps the blade tighter, rubbing her crotch up and down against the man's shuddering thighs. She can tell by the change in vibrations that it's thrust itself past the spinal column and is now splitting him in half, like two legs opening up to receive a welcome lover. The knife blade was forged from the remnants of a meteor, and older metals, older than the eldest of the gods themselves, elements not of their alien worlds but of this world. Her world. The blade can split, lengthen, coil. It speaks to her as it throttles and twists through the nerves and spinal cord and cartilage, twisting, spiraling, bucking around and through bone. Sometimes she picks up snatches of radio whispers in the air. She doesn't know what it's saying. She doesn't care.

Now the man's legs are buckling—he pitches forward, down and to the side, his head slamming against the edge of the desk as he collapses to the floor. Alex rides the body's descent, letting go of the pen and knife handle as she steadies herself so she doesn't fall off. The chair rolls backward, leaving dark wet tracks in its wake. Now she kneels against his back, the twitching flesh pinned under her strong legs. He never got a chance to scream, poor thing. The pain, though—she can tell by the way his body moves, by the tortured sounds pouring out of his mouth, that he still feels everything. And it's not going away just yet. The knife grows both ways, it can hollow out a human in other ways. Alex lifts her skirt again, moving herself over the handle until the tip brushes against the crotch of her panties. She moves her legs over to his sides, pinning his torso in place, and places her hands against his upper back to keep him in place. Already the handle is tearing through the cotton, drilling its way through the folds of her wet flesh; and her entire body shakes in unison with the man as the knife delivers to both of them equal amounts of pleasure and pain.

Her eyesight darkens; the office disappears. In her orgasmic vision, Alex is the blade, splintering into a hundred silver threads, burrowing and whisking its way throughout the man, burning the magic out of his flesh, blending his insides into viscous mush that leaks through his splitting skin and pours over her hands and legs. All the colors of the underworld, flowing between her engorged lips into her body and mind. The burnt smell of superheated blood and crushed bone fills the air. Flashes of antediluvian light, flickering births of supernovas and star nurseries, strobe the images away: she is so close this time, so close to seeing what is there beneath all this shallow surface of sticky, repulsive physical life. Something waits for her down there, beneath the chaotic horror of biologic creation. Eyes that are not eyes, lifting up; thoughts that are not thoughts, turning to her. And it knows her name. A cave; the first cave; the first vein; the first geologic moment in time; the pre-biologic heartbeat of the first life. She is falling, rushing down, breaking apart, plummeting like the Leonids onto the face of—

He's dead.

"Fuck." The word comes out of her mouth on the tide of a low groan—she's stuck on the blade handle, again. Liquefied human goo gels and cools against her skin. The man's body is nothing more than a squishy flat bundle of clothing and skin, everything else covers the office floor like the blackened, pureed remains of restaurant garbage coagulating in a back alley. "Gross," Alex mutters as she arches her back and carefully lifts herself off of the now normal-sized knife handle. Her skirt and blouse are caked and heavy with blood and sweat and coarse bits of bone and viscera—not that it matters, she can explain all that away by saying she had an accident while restocking the production shelves. But she wasn't prepared for this, it was so spur-of-the-moment; and now she'll have to budget more money for the laundry service, which means less money for whiskey come payday. Also, she can't stand the smell.

Grabbing the edge of the desk for support, she pulls herself up onto her shaking legs. Sweat pours down her body, every inch. She's absolutely soaked. "Fuck," she says again, running her fingers over her face and flicking the excess drops into the air. Alex looks down and sighs. She's never going to get this cleaned up, not in a million years. Maybe if she wipes her shoes off on some corner of the carpet that isn't soaking wet with shit and blood, she can leave the room and lock it behind her; no one will know she was ever in here. Not that it matters, she'll have her desk cleaned out by the end of the day. Not that *that* matters, anyway. This is her last day anywhere.

Her mug lies next to the man, coated in goo. Using her finger as a hook, she lifts it by its handle. The straw rattles against the empty plastic sides. What a disappointing sound.

"I need more vodka."

"No, you do not."

Alex drops the cup and turns: a second man steps from the dark of the elevator and raises a gun. Before she can even gasp, he fires. She feels the bullet enter her upper chest, just above her left breast—she's never experienced such terrible pain and force before, even from the blade, perhaps because this is so divorced from numinous mystery, the bullet is just an ordinary piece of metal, poorly forged out of some shallow surface cave passing itself off as a mine: the offensive, naked nothingness of the act takes her breath away. Or maybe that's just the bullet nicking the top of her lung. Alex falls back, down, her head hitting the chair and sending it skittering away as she lands on what's left of the first man's mushy head.

The second man steps out of the elevator, gun leveled at her head now. She has no doubt he can make his mark. She stares over at her knife. It's so close, it only needs her touch—

"No. Stay right where you are," he says, and steps over to the pile of clothes, his gaze and the barrel of the gun never wavering. "Do. Not. Move." He reaches down.

"No..." The word is more of a strangled gasp that doesn't fully leave her mouth.

The man lifts the knife by the tip of the handle, his mouth grimacing as though he's holding a turd. The knife has shrunk back down into its very ordinary shape of all-purpose kitchen tool. He's wearing black gloves, Alex notices, not leather but some type of material that glistens like oil. The sight of those repulsive gloves against her knife, her beloved—despite the pain of moving, a small sob escapes her throat.

"Give it back!"

The man shakes his head as he holds it up, examining the minute carvings on the handle.

"My father's—I'm dying—please just let me hold it until I'm dead."

The man shoots her a look. Alex can't tell if he's amused or sad. "I don't think so."

"I'm not alone—my coworkers—they're calling the police right now."

"You better hope they aren't," he says with a very earnest look on his face, waving the blade back and forth at the mess on the floor. "Although, I'd love to hear your explanation for all of this. I don't think it would work as well as when you took care of your art director. Who happened to also work for me. In the Ministry."

Alex stares at him. She feels all the blood draining from her face in a cold rush, as if she were a child caught with her hands in the candy jar.

"Yes." The man finally moves the gun away, holding his jacket open as he stows the knife. "Anyway, no one on this floor can hear anything that happens in this office. It was built that way. There is some serious fucking magic coating these walls."

"Please, just give me the knife and leave. I won't follow you."

"You can't follow me. The elevator is operated by a key. I am that key, so to speak—it only works for me. Just like the knife only works for you. Same principles, different systems of magic."

"The knife isn't magic. I can't do magic."

"Oh, I know." He sits down at the edge of the desk, looming over her like a thin vulture. His skin is the wane, light brown that occurs when someone goes years without setting foot outdoors, and his jet black hair is pulled back in a neat ponytail, which makes his face and long nose appear even sharper. He really does look like a vulture, one of those Andean condors that sometimes circle over the mists of the Becher in the early morning. His handsome head would look lovely in her refrigerator, or perhaps on her wall, next to the other masks.

"It's not our magic, what you and this knife do," he continues. "Not Obsidian, not elder magic."

"It's not magic," Alex repeats in a dull voice. He thinks he's just going to let her bleed out while he lectures her into her grave. But this isn't how she's going to die. This wasn't what she saw. And perhaps he doesn't know what she can do, without the knife. *Keep talking, you stupid fuck.*

"I think," he says, a thoughtful tone creeping into his words, "I think that perhaps you might be right. In which case, what you are and what you can do is far more troubling than people might suspect."

Alex looks away, out the windows. He can kill her, or not. She's done with him.

"Do you want your knife back?"

She says nothing. Outside, the skies have turned an angry grey. Thunderstorms, or something worse. The air traffic has subsided, but the sirens still wail, wail, wail.

"Yes. I want it back."

"You know you're not dying. I know that, too."

"Yes." Already Alex feels the bullet twirling around in her angry flesh, working its way toward the surface. It's not the bullet's doing—it's her body, pushing it out and knitting up all the damage along the way. Broken bones, a busted nose, cuts and scrapes, a liver and kidneys that never bear the burden of all the booze she drinks. It always ends the same, she emerges from chymical "accidents" and fires as damaged as the corpses she leaves behind; and then she heals and goes on the same as before. It's not magic, though. She's not immortal or indestructible, just— something else, a creature with no power over her own continual re-creation. If it was magic, if she could truly change her flesh on her own, the things she'd do to herself, oh the incredible things…

"You thought you'd just keep me here, talking until you healed yourself, and then? And then?"

Alex smiles. Despite the discomfort, she shrugs.

The man aims the gun and shoots her in the right shoulder.

"You *BITCH*!" Alex slams back against the floor, writhing in pain.

"My apologies." He sets the gun down on the desk, and gingerly steps through the remains of his coworker. "You should know, and I don't expect you to appreciate or thank me for this—" he leans down, grabs her right wrist, and begins dragging her across the floor, speaking loudly over her howls, "—but I was instructed to kill you and toss your body off the building. Which I would have been happy to do if I was working solely for the Ministry. But as it happens—" the man props her up against the back of the elevator, and pulls a large oval clasp, not unlike the clasp of a necklace, out of a discrete panel in the steel wall "—I additionally report to a second organization, and I have another, better use for you. So I need to keep you safe and calm and out of harm's way."

The man unlatches the clasp and lifts up her left wrist.

"Are you ready for this?" he asks.

"I'm going to kill you," Alex says. Her voice is dull and flat, but she injects every bit of hatred inside her into each syllable. "Even if I have to tear my hand off to get to you."

"I don't doubt that. In fact, I'm counting on it." The man

slides the edge of the hook through the middle of her wrist, carefully and expertly nudging it past her shifting bones. Alex feels a dizzying darkness crinkling around the edges of her eyesight, but she doesn't turn away. Blood streams down her arm in thick rivulets, but not enough to indicate that he's hit any major veins or arteries. He's good, he's probably had a lot of practice. The edge of the clasp emerges from the other side of her wrist like a sewing needle, and the man closes the other end of the clasp against its bloody counterpart. It locks with a wet click.

"Why do you drink so much?" the man asks as he steps away, inspecting his handiwork. Alex does the same, staring up at her arm. The clasp is attached to a slender, almost cheap-looking chain that leads up to the recess in the elevator wall. She could rip it out in a second, if her wounds were fully healed. If she wanted. If she gave any fucks at all, which she really does not anymore. A tiny tube winds through the links, she notes, running down the chain and disappearing into the base of the clasp—the light in the elevator is low, but if she squints, she can just make out drops of clear liquid sliding down the tubing. A slow lovely warmth is spreading throughout her limbs, lapping away the sharp edges of the pain. The tube contains alcohol. He didn't miss her veins at all.

"Don't worry, it's not enough to kill you—there isn't

enough vodka in all of Obsidia for that. It's just enough to keep you very content, very docile."

"You're a piece of shit. Tell that to both your employers."

"I've noticed that you're drunk almost all the time at work. Except, of course, when you're taking some poor soul apart like a roast chicken. But then, that's after hours. You're always sober for that. For most people, it's the opposite."

"I'm not most people."

"I noticed that, too."

"And I don't get drunk at work, it's just, it's always just enough to not—never mind. I don't know why you're asking a question you already have the answer to." Alex feels almost gregarious now, despite her desperate inner efforts to care even a single fucking bit about how much she's going to enjoy riding his pulverized bones to the hidden center of the planet and beyond.

"I wanted to make sure you understood why I'm doing this."

"Because I can't heal as fast if I'm drunk. Because you know I'll just sit here like a wet rag doll, sucking up all this free top-shelf booze, pissing myself and dreaming the afternoon away so you can do—" she waves her free arm back and forth in the air "—whatever it is you've come here to do."

"Trust me, it's not top shelf."

Alex smiles. Little bits of dried blood flake off her lips and settle onto her blouse. The man returns the gesture, revealing a wide, clean set of ivory teeth.

"Why is the building shaking so hard?" Alex asks. His polite smile freezes, just a touch. "Why were so many aircraft lifting equipment and machines out of the center of the city? Why was all the traffic this morning so crushing and relentless? All in one direction. I got off in the middle of the spur, but the rest, they just kept going. Thousands and thousands of horses and cars. Should I have gone with them? Here's a more interesting question: why did you stay behind?"

As if in response to her words, dark shadows well up throughout the office as the light retreats from the windows. The blood and carnage fade with the furniture into a soft, uniform gloom.

"Storm," the man says. All the warmth has bled from his voice. "A storm is coming. It's almost here."

"Must be one hell of a storm."

"Yes."

Despite the warmth of the vodka rolling through her veins, cold veins of dread erupt in her chest. "Is this the biggest storm? From the Southern Ocean?"

"Not that one, no. They—haven't found Him yet. He's

still an undiscovered country, dreaming. This is something else. But, also from below."

"Below Becher?" The cold horror doesn't fade away. "Below us?"

His voice is almost a whisper—in the hot gloom, she can barely hear him speak. "Yes."

"What is it?"

"We're not sure." His tone is hesitant. "We can't quite make out its full form."

"And yet we're bringing it up?"

"Yes."

"Which part of Becher is it under?"

He says nothing.

"Which part? Where is it buried?"

"It's not buried, actually. It's being born. We're just— speeding the process up a bit. No, that's not really accurate. More like an immense cesarean, and we're performing the surgery."

"You didn't answer my question: which part of Becher?"

Again, he says nothing.

"Answer me, you fuck!"

The man steps back out of the elevator, and slides the metal gate shut. "I have some work to do on this floor. I'll be back for you in several hours. You'll be fine in here, it's air-conditioned, it's completely safe." He grabs the handle of the closet door.

"Which fucking part of Becher? Which *FUCKING* part?"

He smiles at her again, his pale face a hundred diamonds grimacing behind the steel mesh as he opens his mouth; and Alex almost cries out for him to stop, because she knows what he's going to say and she can't stand it, she's known it all this time, from the moment she woke up in the dead of night, from the moment that massive, mysterious quake momentarily sucked all life out of the earth and sky and replaced it with flat cosmic nothingness, from the moment she put her hand on the great glass panels of the front lobby and pushed her way through the sticky primordial gloom into the dying elevator that wriggled its way up all those shivering, sickly floors to the dilated and curetted rooms of her emptied-out employer in a district emptied out to make way for the even greater vastation of what's coming.

And the door shuts and the darkness covers her completely, leaving only his magic-charged words illuminating the space with their terrible, wondrous fire: *ALL OF IT.*

TENEBROSUS

Eventually, the motes of glowing dust that made up those three small words float apart, settle in the corners of the elevator like the bioluminescent afterglow of a low tide. The building shakes steadily, every now and then giving out an extra hard shudder that sends the elevator rocking back and forth. Alex closes her eyes. Her pinned arm and hand are numb, all the nerves long dead. At some point, she hears the clink of the bullets hitting the floor, one after the other, as her body finishes pushing them out. There's a part of her that feels relief, but it's a million miles beneath her surface, and quickly fades as the excruciating pain in her right wrist takes over in its place. Her aching body moves back and forth between tortured wakefulness and a deliciously languid landscape of fever dreams. The shimmering words become the high towers of a far-off city trapped in an endless night; and she lies at the edge of a great precipice, unable to travel to her final destination, unable to do anything except watch the city burn and glow with power and life while she can only cower at a great distance, alone and eternally separate. Her hand is stretched out to it, to the place she calls home, the quiet sun-drenched rooms, the soft carpets and couch, the jangle of the chimes brushing the edges of the open windows. She's reaching out, but there's so much pain—too much, it's like her bones are breaking over and over again. Alex cries out, her tears mingle with the sweat drenching her face, and a fear-fueled thought sluggishly surfaces as she realizes what's happening: her body is repairing itself once again. The clasp is moving through her wrist, the bones and tendons and muscles breaking down and pushing it through, centimeter by centimeter.

A drowsy sensation of victory washes over her. Alex slides down the wall onto the floor, her entire body limp with relief. Ignoring her arm, now furiously alternating between unendurable pain and blood-drained numbness, she feels unconsciousness stealing over her, righteous and deep.

And then, for a wonderful too-short while, there is nothing—no pain, no fear, not even the dark.

She wakes on her back, cradling her left arm across her stomach. The still-trembling elevator is now pitch black: the phosphorous words have died out. All sense of time has left her—whether it is still afternoon or evening, she has no way of knowing. Tentatively, she runs her fingers over her wrist. The flesh is tender and swollen, and she can make out the deep furrows on both sides of the wrist where the metal was extruded. But her fingers detect the semi-soft beginnings of scabs starting to form over the pulpy wounds. She's still drunk, but her body is healing in its own unfathomable way.

After some rather heated inner debate, Alex rises shakily to her feet, feels her way to a corner of the elevator opposite the metal gate, and urinates. The act thoroughly disgusts her, but she doesn't have a choice—the man left her no better off than a caged animal. *You have nothing to be ashamed of,* she tells herself as she struggles to pull up her underwear and smooth down the ruins of her skirt. *When you've finished hollowing him out with the knife, you can shit on the remains of his face and see how much he complains.*

She makes her way to the gate, running her hands over the metal in search of a lock, then extends her search to the walls on either side of it. No lock, no panels or controls. She pushes her fingers through the grating, but the wooden door is out of reach. Remembering the small recess that the chain and tubing ran out of, Alex feels her way across the back of the elevator, but finds nothing. After several minutes, her hands detect the seams of the small door. How did the door close on its own—did the chain retract once the clasp left her hand? The elevator only worked for him, Alex remembers the man saying. More bullshit Obsidian magic. She makes her way to the corner opposite her puddle of urine, and slides down to the floor. How long? He said he would return. The rhythmic shaking of the building sends her back into a drowsy state, but beneath the daydreams and ghost-like thoughts of her semi-sleep, she feels her strength returning, she feels her cold desires blossoming. Normally it's months before she feels the urge to explore again, but the world has been reduced to a set of mammoth circumstances beyond her control, that are squeezing and pushing against her like the Nazca Plate, continually crashing against the entire length of Obsidia. She has no choice but to push back.

The doorknob turns. Alex bolts up and presses against the back of the elevator. Dim light slowly washes through the space as the wooden door opens. The man stands before the gate, jacket and tie gone, his formerly white shirt black with blood. A large gash runs down the side of his face.

Alex raises her left hand.

"Ah. Of course. I should have known. You're remarkable."

"Which of my coworker's blood is on your shirt?"

"Everyone's. Well, almost everyone's." The man holds her mug up to the gate, working a straw through the holes. "My name is Diogenes, by the way. I have water, if you'd like. I'm sure you're thirsty."

"Is it spiked?"

Diogenes shakes his head. "I need your particular talents, and for that I need your head clear. Two of your coworkers have proven particularly adept at avoiding me, as well as extra-resistant to our chymical agents—you wouldn't have noticed, because they'd have no effect on you at all, but the air here on the fortieth floor is currently full of all kinds of wonderful things, whispering in everyone's ear, *go to the elevator lobby, something extraordinary waits for you in the beautiful anchor room*."

"You're a fucking idiot. Doesn't your branch of the Ministry know? Magic doesn't work on us. That's why we all work at the press, so we can duplicate the books and grimoires without accidentally or purposely making the spells work."

Diogenes sighs as if speaking to an annoying child. "*Most* magic doesn't work on *some* of you. Magic attracts magic, which is why we didn't need this level of supervision for the other thirty-nine floors. All of those employees have entered their anchor rooms—their elevator lobbies— willingly, many of them joyfully. However, the Ministry concocted something special, something a bit more complex yet subtle for the employees of the fortieth floor, to make everyone more compliant. It was a gamble—and it paid off, for the most part. There were, unfortunately, some side effects." He grimaces and points to his shirt. "This was

Bartram."

"You need my help finding them, don't you. You need my help killing them. Why are you doing this if the entire district is about to be destroyed anyway?"

"That's actually not going to happen. You know more than anyone, transformation doesn't always result in death."

"What do you mean?"

Alex waits for him to elaborate, but the man remains stubbornly quiet. "Fine," she finally says. "But what's in it for me if, after I help you, you're just going to toss me off the building like you said you would?"

"I said I'd toss you off the building, I didn't say that I'd kill you. And, I'll return your knife to you—which I've deposited in a safe place, accessible only by me, by my actual living essence and not a body part, so don't get any ideas—after you complete the kills. I need actual bodies, not rivers of mush running down the walls. So, no precious knife. You can use a regular knife, just like a regular psychopath. It'll be a new experience for you, it might be fun."

Alex looks down at the floor. She doesn't want to admit how she feels, how good it sounds, how strong and weak in the knees she's getting at the thought of hunting down those annoying, whiny, lazy, disrespectful fucks. She doesn't want to give in. And yet. And yet.

"You know you want to." Diogenes' voice is a low, seductive whisper, curling around inside her brain. "You can feel that urge rising inside. Like an engine, coming to hot life, all those pistons pumping up and down, gathering purpose. If Becher is coming to an end as we know it, why not give in? What's stopping you? Certainly not me. Do what you were born to do, one last time."

Alex moves to the gate, her fingers curling around the grating. "We meek little publishing bookworms aren't as compliant a lot, aren't as 'docile' as you thought."

"Oh, no, most of you were extremely compliant—the agent did exactly as we'd hoped, for the most part. Two of your coworkers, however, are actually natural adepts, which we didn't realize until today. They've been passing themselves off as mundane-born with minimal thauma-ported augmentation, which means the chymicals are having almost no reaction on them. I'm not able to counter whatever protection they're casting out. Ironic, isn't it? Especially considering *your* circumstances. That's some amazing handiwork, by the way." Diogenes points to the fake thauma-port made of her own bones and skin, still clinging to her throat with tiny stitches made from a spider-thin thread woven out of her own hair and harvested veins, so that her body will never reject or push it off.

Alex frowns. "Never mind my circumstances. Let me guess: Vecula is one of the two remaining, isn't she?"

"Yes. Southern Ocean born, a hybrid child of the sunken city. Her mother was a descendent of one of the original human child sacrifices to Mother Hydra, and on her father's side—well, the phrase 'it's turtles all the way down' applies, if you catch my drift. She thinks she's a mundane, but her magical abilities are actually of a different magnitude and nature altogether, which is why the agent isn't working on her. Amazingly stupid girl, though. I mean, it's really quite shocking how idiotic she is."

"Well, she's managed to avoid you so far, so clearly she's smarter than you. Who's the other?"

If the man is insulted, he doesn't show it. "Felix Pitts."

A great, orgasmic burst of joy rocks her entire body.

"Can I cut out his heart?"

Diogenes cocks his head. "Um, well, you aren't going to eat it or do something weird with it, are you?"

"Don't be disgusting. No. I just want to hold it in my hands."

Diogenes slides open the gate and holds out her mug. Alex takes it.

5:08 PM

Alex moves down the familiar halls in silence, almost in reverence. She's spent her entire adult life working here— she was hired before graduating first in her class from the small trade school in northern Obsidia, in a district so overflowing with all the colossal detritus and abandoned machinery of the continent, that it was simply known as Midden, its original name long forgotten. She remembers the first time she walked these halls, the bookshelves still empty and gleaming with polish, the floors unstained and bright, all the windows dust-free and positively brilliant with the light of a younger sun. Everyone was so excited to be there. Bartram was young and thin and had all his hair, Quartus was a charming and rather sexy silver fox of a mere fifty years—that was thirty years ago. The three of them, they were the first. She's fifty now, and the only one left.

Spatters of blood crisscross the ceiling as they round the corner, and continues all down the long hall, drying in wide swaths on the walls and congealing in thick puddles on the floor. "A woman named Marie," Diogenes says.

"Our copy editor. What did you do to her? That's enough blood up there for a couple of people."

"Some heavy-grade casting. It wasn't pretty. She had a

terrible reaction to the chymicals. Her body started growing, and then she began to—I guess 'ingest' is the best word, or maybe 'absorb,' small machinery. I found her merging with a fax machine."

"Don't you still have your gun?"

"No." He sounds sheepish. "The gun was for you, not them. The bullets just deflected off whatever magic everyone was emitting. And then I ran out of bullets, so I threw it at her. She just ate it."

Alex covers her mouth to hide her sudden urge to laugh. "I thought the Ministry did a better job of training its assassins than this."

"I'm not an assassin, I'm a thaumaturgical engineer in the Ministry of Obstetrics. Chymical warfare and hand-to-hand-or-whatever combat is not my strong suit, obviously."

"Obviously. Please don't tell me what happened to anyone else, especially Bartram. He was already looking terrible when I last saw him this morning. I don't even want to imagine what happened to him by the time you got to him."

"For someone who loves to kill people the way you do, you draw an odd line in the sand."

"We all have our limits. We don't get to choose them."

"You really thought I was an assassin? That's quite a compliment, I'm very flattered."

"Shut the fuck up."

They continue in silence, Diogenes directing her through the labyrinth of rooms with complete ease. Magic attracts magic, he had said; and he assured her, as she sucked down the water back in the hidden office, that he would be able to find Felix and Vecula easily, that navigating the fickle and changing layout would be as simple as breathing.

"Why can everyone do magic except me?" she blurts out, expecting no answer in return. "Every fucking creature in Obsidia except me. What's wrong with me?"

Diogenes stops walking, and puts a finger to his lips. They're standing just outside the warren of rooms that make up Bartram's small kingdom within a kingdom— Editorial and Copyediting. Alex points to the large set of double wooden doors. Diogenes touches her arm, leads her just around the corner, and bends down. *They're both inside*, he barely breathes into her ear. *Felix is in the largest room, straight ahead of us, Vecula is somewhere off to his left. Don't try to lead them out or draw them into some long conversation, just kill them, then come get me. I've got an eighteen-hundred-hour deadline I have to keep.*

Cutting it a bit close, aren't you? What happens at six?

That rumbling throughout the building? That's the machines, in the basements below the sub-basements. They run the entire length of the spur, in all four spurs. They're just idling now. At six, they all turn on. Get in there, go. I'll be waiting here.

I don't have a weapon.

Half the crap on this floor can be used as a weapon. I know, I've seen your work. Be creative—surprise yourself.

He pushes her back around the corner. Alex walks over to the doors and places her hands on the worn brass handles. Bartram never liked people from other departments just dropping into Editorial unannounced. You always had to make an appointment through Felix, as though you were a stranger, a visitor to LBA Press, there to formally present your progress, pitch your idea, gain permission to use the library, or register your complaint. She pushes down on the long handle, and it makes a loud, clean click. The door swings open effortlessly. If they were using magic to keep it closed, well, now they already know who's entering—Lenkiewicz Belanger Apostolicum's legendarily mundane and apparently always-drunk receptionist. The harmless court jester, that's who.

"Hello?" Alex calls out. "It's Alex. Anybody here?" She doesn't need to make sure she's putting just the right amount of tentative fear into her voice. This is all so natural to her, there's no thought to it at all. She closes the door behind her, making sure she locks it shut. She's in a smaller version of reception, an octagonal room where Felix's desk holds court, with various doors leading to offices, printing and art rooms, and the jewel in the crown, the official LBA library, where thousands of rare and obscure research books and materials sit behind locked bookcase doors. Alex walks quietly over to Felix's desk and swipes the heavy letter opener from the pencil cup. He loves that letter opener; it's an antique with a carved ivory handle covered in little flowers and skulls that he picked up years ago during a vacation to the remains of the Panama Canal. She's always loved it, too. Tucking the opener into the back of her skirt, she also picks up a sharp No. 2 pencil, heads for the library door, opens it, and peers inside, every inch of her trembling as if expecting a sudden blow. The lights are on, illuminating long wooden tables and chairs. The shelves are bare: every single bookcase is open, the lead-lined glass doors glinting under the soft lights. Not even a stray Post-It in sight.

"Alex?"

She turns, pressing her back flat against the wall as she raises the pencil in the air like a weapon.

"Alex." The door to Bartram's office swings open a crack, and Felix's face peers out from the dark interior. "Holy fuck, I thought you were dead, too."

"Felix, is that you?" Alex takes a single step forward, but doesn't lower her arm. "Are you okay? What the fuck happened, where is everyone?"

"Come in, come in, quick!" He opens the door and motions for her to come inside. She runs around the desk and sidles past him, her back against the door, and then against the wall of Bartram's office. All the lights are off, and it's as dark outside as if it were midnight, with only a faint glow indicating the presence of Obsidia surrounding the now completely dark district. All those people, Alex realizes as she walks over to the windows, all those homes and businesses surrounding the outer edges of Becher River. They have no idea what's coming. Millions of people right outside the district are also going to die tonight, an ouroboros of carnage rising in their place.

"What the fuck happened to you?" Felix asks as he locks the door behind them. He places a hand over his mouth, as if horrified. Alex realizes what she must look like to him, clothes coated in drying gore, hair matted with blood, open wounds and bruises all across her body like ripe plums.

"Are you alone? Is anyone else alive?"

"Vecula—she's in Bartram's bathroom. She's been in there ever since this started, I can't get her to come out. Right after the editorial meeting, everyone started getting really sick—just, terrible magic, it was horrifying."

"But you're okay?"

"Me and Vecula, we're fine. I tried to get help, but none

of the phones work, the entire elevator lobby is infected with this green lava-like fire, and no one could find the emergency exits. They just fucking disappeared!"

"What green fire?"

"I don't know!" Felix shouts. "Who cares, it's just like, it's—and then this man, he appeared out of nowhere, he just started killing everyone, for no reason!"

"Mother Hydra help us."

"Alex, what happened, where have you been all this time?"

"I—I'm not sure what happened, exactly," Alex begins, tears starting to slide down her cheeks. She takes a step forward, letting the pencil drop to her feet. It clatters and rolls away under Bartram's desk. "I woke up in that little office, it was just maybe half an hour ago. I was so drunk, I must have just passed right out. I woke up, and I heard someone in the hallway, I thought maybe it was you, but it was some stranger, some man in a suit, I don't know, and then—" she stops to swallow a sob, "—he saw me and started chanting in some language I've never heard, and he had this piece of metal in his hand, I didn't know what to do. He lunged at me, he tried to hit me with it, and I just—just started grabbing whatever I could off the shelves and throwing it at him. Books, weights, I hit him with glass jars, I cut him, he was bleeding all over. But he wouldn't stop, and then, I'm so stupid, I remembered my knife—" she raises her skirt slightly, revealing the leather straps "—and I started stabbing and stabbing until he stopped moving—" her voice drops to a whisper. Felix rushes up to her, grabbing her upper arms.

"I killed him." Shivering, Alex lets go of her skirt: one hand slides up under her blouse as she squeezes Felix's shoulder for support.

"Is he dead? Are you absolutely certain?"

"Yes, I'm certain. His eyes were open, but he wasn't moving. He looked shocked. Like this." She slides the letter opener up and thrusts it into his chest. "Yes, that's exactly what the man looked like. Like he had no idea how much he underestimated me."

Felix slides silently to his knees, then topples over. Alex pushes him onto his back, and pulls the opener out, then raises it. "Do not move."

In the bathroom doorway, Vecula freezes like a baby guanaco before a jaguar, her slender pale limbs trembling as she presses herself up against the frame.

"Did you do all of this?" she asks.

"No. Just Felix. In exchange for my life. Well, he doesn't know that part of the exchange yet." Alex steps forward, wiping the blade of the letter opener against her arm as she slowly makes her way toward the girl.

Vecula darts a glance at the door, but Alex can tell she knows it's too far.

"And what would I need to give you in exchange for my life?"

"That's a good question. Except, you're not going to like the answer. I already know that some massive creature is under Becher, and it's going to be born and destroy the entire district. I also know that that man waiting out in the hallway is just like you and Felix, and he knows you're in here, just like you probably know he's out there, right? You can sense each other, some magic crap like that, right?" Vecula only stares down at her bare feet, spattered with droplets of blood like rubies across the webbing and pale pink polish. "He's waiting for me to kill you so he can use your body. For what, I have no idea."

"I know."

Alex stops in her tracks.

"If I tell you, will you let me go?"

"You can't get off the floor."

"There's a terrace on the thirty-fifth floor—there's a terrace every five floors down. Each one circles the entire building. Say I jumped out the window before you could catch me."

"That's insane. You'll die."

"You have no idea what I can do." A small tone of

haughtiness creeps into her voice. "You all think I'm so stupid, and maybe I am, maybe I don't know anything about stupid books, but I know things. I know magic, and it's not crap. I also know that by the end of this evening, this entire building is going to be turned into a pillar of thaumaturgical fire, and all of the spurs are going to rise up straight into the air and those beams are going to point right down all across Becher and completely pulverize every inch of rock beneath it, and then this entire district is going to drop over ten kilometers down into the earth and attach itself to the top of whatever's down there, and then those spurs and all that machinery in Becher are going to drag Becher and that thing back up the walls to the surface. Becher isn't going to be destroyed because it's not a district. It's a gigantic round forceps."

Alex lowers her arm. "What. The. *FUCK.*"

Vecula smiled. "I know, right? My dad told me. Half of the equipment in the spurs was made by his company. He tells me all kinds of shit he's not supposed to, because he thinks living above the surface has made me so stupid that I can't understand anything he says anymore. He calls me his little oxygen retard, right to my face. Can I go now?"

She's going to escape, the little princess, she's going to sail off into the night and across the river, and leave us all here for her beautiful, magic-filled life. She'll spend the rest of her days talking about her ugly, slow coworkers—especially the monstrously tall, scarred receptionist she duped into letting her escape. Or maybe the story will be a terrible fight, with bolts of magic crackling in the air, the vanquished and broken woman collapsing in a heavy heap at the lithe enchantress's perfect feet. Or bowing and genuflecting, licking her oceanic mistress like a whipped dog. Vecula won't say anything with malice, she is genuinely too stupid for such an emotion. But she'll rewrite the tale, and she'll believe it, and so will everyone who hears it. Unless.

"Yes, you can leave," Alex says. She walks over to the nearest window and unlocks the heavy brass latches. Warm, wet air flows in as she pulls the heavy glass pane into the room. Vecula still stands near the doorway.

"Come on, quick, while there's still time." Alex holds her hand out, and Vecula darts across the room, embracing her in a hard hug. "Thank you *so* much, I promise I'll pay you back someday!"

"You're going to pay me back right now." Alex whips the girl around and presses her against the wall, pinning her slender frame with her entire body. Vecula writhes underneath her, but it seems almost half-hearted.

"I knew you'd want more," Vecula says, sounding almost coquettish. "Everyone above the surface always wants more.

No one's happy with what they were born with. It's going to get all of you in so much trouble someday. You're going to find the god you're all looking for, and you'll wake him up, and you'll never be able to put him back to sleep."

"You weren't happy with what you were born with, either." Alex runs the tip of the letter opener along the rows of sharp diamonds at Vecula's throat. Tiny clicks fill the hot air. "Do these come from the depths of the Southern Ocean, too?"

"They came from another world." Vecula begins to weep.

"Well, then. Maybe it's time you learned your own lesson."

Vecula's high-pitched screams don't stop her, or move her. What has moved her in her miserable life? Sitting in the light of the setting sun, watching the single cube of ice melt in the amber liquid she holds in her long crooked fingers? A towel, folded into the shape of Lady Slipper's flower, resting at the foot of her black iron oven? Standing at her window, watching the glittering witches of the underworld float to and fro across the wet cobblestone alleys? These things make her calm, give her a semblance of normality and balance, but they don't move her. Alex suspects what moves her lies perhaps in another universe, in the cosmic depths she can never quite reach in her kills.

After she finishes skinning Vecula's neck, Alex gently lifts her unconscious body up and slides her over the sill, then closes the window. What she would give to know the story the girl will tell now, she wonders as she coils the wet strands of diamond-studded flesh around her fingers, then slips them off and shoves them into her bra. As she leaves Bartram's office, Alex places the letter opener back into Felix's chest, and gives it an extra shove. She never wanted to look at his heart. She always knew exactly what was inside.

5:46 PM

"I still can't believe you let her go," Diogenes says as they quickly wheel Felix down the hallway. His stiffening body is draped over one of the plastic carts the press uses—used to use—to transport the larger manuscripts and supplies from one office to another. It was Alex's suggestion, after Diogenes declared he was too wiped out to haul one more pound of flesh through what seemed like miles of corridor.

"I can't believe you trusted me."

"I can't believe that myself, to be honest. But I figured I'd get at least one body out of it."

"Mine, right?"

"That was a possibility. But, no. Hate always wins out

over love. And your hate for them was greater than theirs for you."

"Do you really believe that? That hate wins?"

"Yes. But, I believe that kind of hate is almost a kind of love. How are you feeling?"

"Fine. I mean, tired. A bit shell-shocked. But, I'm fine. Why?"

"Reception is just up ahead, right?"

"Yes, right down there, at the end of the hall. If it hasn't moved, again."

"Nothing in this building will ever move again. All of the configurations are now locked and in perfect alignment."

"Because of the beam of fire, right?"

Diogenes looks surprised.

"Vecula knew. Her father owns some, or all, of the factories that made the machines that are going to start the spurs. He told her everything. She told me everything. It's some kind of traction beam, right? A suspension system for lowering and raising Becher."

"Interesting. Well, I guess it's good that you let her go. I can't imagine what her father would do if she'd died. No doubt his power is vast and otherworldly."

Alex bites her lower lip.

"Anyway. This is what's going to happen. I'm going to wheel him into reception, while right now, you're going to take this—" Diogenes stops the cart, reaches into his pocket, and takes out a small plastic building security badge "—and you're going back to the elevator in the Ministry office and riding it up to the roof. That's where I put your knife. Just press the barcoded side of the badge against the right side of the gate, and you'll see your floor options displayed. No magic required, it's all high tech."

"You said the elevator could only—yeah. Of course. Well played."

He smiles.

"And that's it? I can just leave? Where are you going to be?"

"I need to put this body into the anchor room—which is no longer just your elevator bank. It's a single column extending from the machine room below the sub-basements all the way up to the roof, and it runs, in part, on biological materials. Every body in the building is necessary. Including mine. What happens to you won't be of any concern to me."

"That doesn't bother you, that you'll die? Why don't you just walk away, or run?"

"It's not in my nature to run—and it is in my job description to finish my assignment."

"Which job?"

Diogenes raises an eyebrow. "Actually, both. But I'm not going to die. This is simply another transformation. Who knows what's on the other side? Maybe it's Obsidia again, or a different version of Obsidia, or something else. I'm sure the Ministry knows, but they wouldn't give us the particulars. I'm very much looking forward to finding out." Diogenes grabs the cart handle and starts pushing. "Go on, you don't have much time, unless you plan on sticking around, or getting back to the first floor like Vecula did." He gives her a little shove. "Go on, fly away. I have faith in you."

Alex turns and runs back down the hallway, praying she'll find the office quickly. So many fucking manuscripts, papers sliding all over the floors, spilled ink and viscous fluids—did he have to destroy the entire office in order to kill nine employees? "He really wasn't an assassin," she mutters, kicking aside a copper funerary jar. A soft plume of grey ash explodes as it bounces off a bookcase, coating her ankles with human dust as she passes through it. The door, there it is, just down the hallway to her right. Alex doesn't even know what part of the floor she's on, whether it's south or west or north. But a scattering of lights appears at the horizon through the windows, orienting her. She's facing north now, away from the district and out over Obsidia. Picking her way across the now thoroughly congealed mass of flesh her beloved blade left behind, Alex grabs the closet door handle and slams it shut behind her as she steps into the elevator. Instantly, she's plunged into pure black.

"Card, card." Alex slams it against the right side of the gate. Nothing. "Other side, other side." She flips it and tries again. Nothing. God-shitting lying son of a bitch. Her hand reaches blindly out and smashes into the gate. The gate! She slams it closed, then hits the wall with the card again. Lights flood the elevator, and the gate automatically locks. A series of numbers appear within the wall, glowing bright red. She presses her fingertip hard against R, and the elevator lurches up. Alex keeps the badge against the wall as she studies the rest of the display. L for lobby, B for basement. SB must be sub-basement. The floors listed below, though: SB1, SB2, SB3, SB4—all the way to SB14. And then: RB. Alex shivers. River Bottom. If only she had had more time...

The door pings, and the gate slides open, revealing a standard metal door, vibrating along with the building. Slipping the badge into her skirt pocket, Alex pushes the door. It swings out to a vast, flat rooftop. In the center, a massive column of cool green fire is streaming out and into the sky, a reverse waterfall of pure magic. She looks up. She sees no end, there is no sign of the column bending or arcing, falling back under its own weight onto itself or across Becher. It simply goes on forever. Alex turns around in a slow circle. From here the entire district spreads out, a dead zone, black as oil, its edges discernable only by the faint sickly glow of the river; and the three other spurs. Each one is lit up like a candle, the single highest building at each apex shooting the same pale-green column of fire into the black sky. The black sky over Becher, that is: far across the river, miles away, Obsidia still glimmers under the late afternoon sun. Alex stares again into the dark sky. Is it the sky? Is it their sky, or are those obsidian clouds from someplace else?

She rubs her eyes, and starts loping alongside the railing. No time to think about any of this, she has to find her knife. Alex runs her hands along the metal rails, praying for a bit of the blade. Even in the glow of the fire, it's almost impossible to see each individual bit of steel. But where else would he have put it? She reaches the southeast edge and heads north, working her hand over every bit of metal as if she were making love to it. It's only when she's halfway up the eastern side that she sees it—a small platform perched in the middle of the northern edge of the railing. Alex runs, her bare feet slapping against the pebbly surface. Yes, she sees it now, her knife standing at attention in the middle of the platform's flat, wooden surface, its point embedded dead center. She reaches out and grabs the handle. Instantly its gentle thrum radiates through her bones like a song. But it won't come out. Alex tugs again, harder. It doesn't budge. She places both hands on the grip, crouches down slightly for better traction, and—

6:00 PM

—the column explodes into a solid mass of roiling thaumaturgical matter. The explosion is so loud her eardrums burst. Alex screams, but she can't hear herself; but it doesn't matter, because now the suction from the force of the fire is lifting her off her feet, sucking her toward the deep green river. She grips the knife handle as tight as she's ever held anything in her entire life. Somewhere, at the other end of her body, her shoes are gone, her skirt is shredding away, her flesh is starting to crackle and blister with fire. And now: the entire railing lurches forward. It's starting. Beyond the massive roar of the fire, an even greater, deeper thunderstorm of machines, as they spring to life. The spurs are lifting. Alex feels her bowels and bladder evacuating, but it's all so far away, her body is nothing, there is no flesh, there is no Alex, there is only the handle, the handle of her beloved that she wills into her flesh, wills into her bones, nailing her to that slender platform that defies the entire maelstrom around it, and the building is lurching upward, and out, out, out, out, and above her the naked half of the spur reaches high toward the baleful skies, and the building is pointing inward, out across the entire district toward the other three, and she can feel her hair burning as the beams smash into each other, the shockwave visible like an airborne tsunami, and now the columns are abhorrent emerald, liquid and alive, they are death and flesh and the river, redirected and scouring the earth beneath Becher away as it begins its unstoppable descent; and she should be dead, she should be ashes but she burns, she burns and hardens like a diamond, like a hideous newly forged blade. And the platform gives way. She flies out and up; and then directly down into the great mother river of birth and destruction, black night giving way into green, into white—

into—

to—

—

AFTER

There is a blackness so tight and complete that all thoughts bleed away into it, all breath, all sound.

And then:

Soft grey veins of cloudy light begin to cut through like

lightning, followed by ripplings of dark purples and blues, little flashes of orange and white, like when she used to rub her eyes as a child and her lids and pupils would press together to create phantom kaleidoscopic landscapes that only she could see. After a while, she realizes she is realizing things, that she is a she, that her eyes are not closed, that she is seeing some terrifying and new place, traveling through it like an infinitesimal mote of dust.

Awareness is followed, slowly, gradually, by sounds. Her breath, moving in and out of her slightly open mouth (she has a mouth! she has a body!), the faint whoosh and thump of blood surging through her heart, the wail of air rushing in and out of her lungs. But the wailing sound gradually shifts, evolves, and with it so does her understanding: it's coming from outside of her, not within. A low colossal moaning that widens into a deep and endless chorus of heart-rending sobs. All around, the landscape brightens, as if some dying sun is rising a universe away. She has hands, and she holds them up in the dim air. Now she has her bearings, her full awareness of self. She is floating, hemmed in on all sides by malformed beings positioned exactly like she is—upright, with feet pointed down toward a distant land that looks like scorched, burned flesh oozing with blisters and open sores.

How long it takes for her to raise and press her fists

against her ears, she has no way of knowing. The wailing is an ocean of tortured screaming now, flowing over and through her, unrelenting and inescapable. Snatches of ancient, malformed words and syllables occasionally surface from out of the aural maelstrom, and her entire body jolts with recognition at each one. This is a song. She feels her jaws and cheeks at the sides of her palms, motionless. Why is she not screaming and singing with them? Why is she not in pain? Why is she aware?

She wills herself upward, in cautious, incremental movements. She must know where she is. Time. There is something called time, and this movement, this breaking from the pack returns it to her fully, as though she is surfacing from another dimension. Faces split in half, jaws hang from dripping heads, eyeless sockets filled with wriggling veins and snapping jaws, heads that are not heads at all but bulbous tumors and contusions and masses of splintered pulp and bone. Squirting tentacles, broken wings and hooves, piston limbs and keyboard smiles. She stares wildly about her, waiting for someone to turn to her, to drag her back down. They stream on, oblivious even as her toes brush the edges of their gaping moist flesh. They stream on, and she hangs above them now, silent, astonished, still.

They are at the jagged edges of a vast cliff that drops off

sharply into a smoking abyss. She and others like her, upright and sailing one after the other like a mindless swarm, thin bodies hanging and drifting in an endless ouroboros of ghouls and ghosts. Thousands. Millions. The swarm is not one layer of beings, but many—too many for her to see their end. The cliff is circular, she can see the curve from either side of her, but it is so wide she cannot see across to the other side. Once again, she floods her body with her will, and she drifts across the great river of spectral pain, until she reaches the edge, daring to go no farther. The sky is brighter now, with huge shafts of light occasionally breaking through from above, illuminating the face of the cliffs. Water and what looks like blood and oil streams from thin orifices, plummeting down the glistening sides—remnants of a once-unstoppable river, she recalls. But beyond the cliffs, so far down she can barely believe what she sees—movement in the flashes of increasing light. Small movements, small buildings, small plumes of green fire, small gyres of cogs. No, not small—merely so far below her that what she now realizes is a wondrously complex and sprawling mechanism of industry and machinery appears spread out below her feet like nothing more than a miniature diorama. And crisscrossing all of this are two fat beams of brilliant emerald fire. The singing and wailing has diminished with the darkness, and she hears and feels the vibrations of the power lines running up through her body, the steady cyclopean pounding of the city, of its heart. This is what sings to her now, and she wants to join.

Her fists are still at her ears, and she feels—yes, this is pain. No, wait, this is only discomfort. There was a true, life-rending pain before the blackness, she remembers, a bone-splintering, flesh-pulverizing sundering that cracked her open and extruded her smashed remains into this place, but this is merely prickly bites all along her fingers and against her palms, mundane in comparison to the cacophony of the world around her. She lowers her hands before her and uncurls her stiff fingers. Coiled inside each palm are several strands of pale-green leather, studded with white diamonds. They are small and delicate and even in the low morning light of this still sunless place, she can see how beautiful and perfect they are, how in the muted dawn they shine and gleam like polished teeth in rows of wide smiling mouths.

I am Alexandria Jessamine.

Memories silently explode throughout her, like brilliant fireworks lighting up a barren sky. Vecula. Felix. Diogenes. Becher. And somewhere in the labyrinthine ruins of all of it, her beloved apartment, and her beloved.

The sun is up now, full and hard and hot like it used to be, except she sees it now not just as a sun but a star in a whorl of stars, she sees all the stars before and behind it in this great arm of their galaxy. She senses the cosmic void behind and around it, but it is not a void at all, it is alive with incomprehensible, terrible, joyous purpose; and her newly forged body is a part of this purpose.

Alex laughs and cries all at once, and the black-chested eagles soaring past serenade her in response. She is dead, and filled with more life than she thought possible. Becher's newly created river of the dead has become a mere shadow to her now, a flickering presence whose painful dirge registers in her ears as a faint but clear warning to those beyond the district's transformed borders: do not pass. And a siren song for the being below, an interdimensional welcoming, a sweet lullaby. It is her siren song, too, her welcome back to a place she never belonged and can seemingly never escape.

Alex wills the strands of diamond and flesh around her wrists—they twist and nestle against her slender wrists, and she raises them in the clear air, admiring how they wink and shine, how the thin strands of electricity that arc off her newly silver fingertips reflect in their faceted faces. Beyond the ouroboros, Obsidia gleams with them: she sees the city as it really exists: radiant, triumphant, a stupendous conglomeration of human-made buildings and immense non-human structures that constantly shift and morph as they flicker from the light of this universe to the next and back again. This is the new city, taking shape all across the ravaged and raped continent, still wet and glistening with the cold abyssal and hadal waters of the Southern Ocean. Alex stares at the horizon, mesmerized. How would it be, to spend eternity floating through it, exploring and discovering its every abhorrent and miraculous secret? How would it be, to add to that terror and wonder with lovely little acts of beauty and terror all her own?

But Alex is a daughter of earth, not Obsidia. The city is eternal; the things she loves and longs for are not. Obsidia can wait. Below her feet, wondrous things are happening, as well as so many things she wanted to do before, in her old life, when she never had the power, time, or nerve.

"There you are." Alex reaches out toward the sky, fingers spread wide. It's blue, a true bright blue, like meadow flowers in the mountains, the blue of swordfish and jaguar eyes and turquoise-capped teeth of the gill-throated women of the Antarctic territories. The blue of the hearts of cenotes and glaciers. The blue of her vision of the moment she dies…

She stares at her fingers. The dark veins of thaumaturgical fire are mere sparks now, and she feels the full weight of her body, the full weight of gravity. "No," she whispers. Of course. She didn't die. Again. She just went through those stupid fucking beams, and ended up here, with all of the truly dead. The magic was never hers—there was no transformation, only vestiges of the power beams coating her corporeal form, keeping her floating and alive. And now it's bled off with the night, and the cliffs are rising up all around her, faster and higher.

"Oh fuck me *no*—" And she's falling, spinning around and around while the black-breasted eagles shriek and dive, and she flips around in the air and sees that sky, sees that bright clear blue she's never seen before in her life and will never see again, she's flying away from it, down and into the animate emerald abyss of Becher, screaming, screaming, screaming...

TUESDAY, AUGUST 26
12:27 PM

Alex wakes up out of death, lets out a single gasp, and freezes. There is so much pain flooding her body that she doesn't dare move or breathe. Not that she thinks she can. She can only stare up at the iron and glass ceiling, at the jagged hole directly overhead, and the dusty grey of the far-off sky.

I'm still alive.

"Welcome back."

The pale image of a man crouches over her, his body flickering in and out like a scratchy strip of movie film. He looks familiar, with long black hair and abyssal-dark eyes. Standing behind him, also peering down at her, are several other men and women, all dressed in similar drab suits, holding small black notebooks and clipboards. Every one of them is scribbling furiously away, except for one older man who is taking photos of her with a very large flash camera. "Diogenes, remember? From M37?" His voice sounds as scratchy and tinny as his visage. "We tracked you all the way to this roof. The fall, that is—we tracked your fall. It was spectacular. When you're feeling a bit better, several of the Ministry's personnel would like to speak with you. About the fall, and other certain aspects of your life. I can be there, if you like. Anyway, when you're ready." He grows silent.

She has to work at it for a minute to get her tongue and jaw gently into position. It feels like all her teeth are still there, but everything feels so raw and new. How could she have survived that fall? Unless, like her beloved knife, she can never die, only break and mend again and again. "Did I die? Didn't we all die?"

"We—" Diogenes turns and looks back at his companions for a quick second. "We can't quite say what happened to you. I mean, the rest of us, everyone else who was in Becher at the time—I wouldn't quite call it 'dead' in the traditional sense. We've merely transitioned into something a bit more useful for this part of the process. As you can see, I seem to still be adjusting, I can't quite get it right..." He looks down at his flickering hands, clearly annoyed.

"Process?"

"Well, now we have to spend the next several centuries making sure Becher District does its job—we have to remain here and keep the engines and spurs working as we move the cargo attached beneath us up the sides of the birthing wall to the surface. This is Epoch II."

Alex says nothing. The building begins to rock back and forth in hard thrusts, and several panes of glass crash from the skylights down onto the floor. The men and women collectively cringe and duck.

"Don't worry," one of the observers pipes up, "this happens all the time now. Every five minutes or so, actually. It'll get smoother once we work the kinks out. After a while, you won't even notice it."

"Every five minutes," Alex murmurs. "For centuries."

"Yes," Diogenes says, his voice lowering. "We still have centuries."

"We need to move her," one of the women says, and Diogenes nods. And then they disappear from Alex's view.

She feels a thin sheet snapping over her naked body, then hands lifting her up. A low howl slides out of her mouth as new waves of pain wash over her. "Sorry," a voice says. The skylights drift from view, replaced by steel girders and a cracked concrete ceiling covered in heavy pulleys and chains. A warehouse.

"Where am I?"

A young man with a very earnest face pops into view. "When you fell, you were pretty close to the edge—you were lucky you didn't slip down between the walls and the district, there's a massive gap and God knows where you would have ended up. Anyway, you're in one of the old warehouse districts that used to line the river. Southwest." Alex feels her body lower back onto the floor. If only she could roll her eyes. Didn't they even bother to bring a stretcher? Fucking government workers, everything always on the cheap. Diogenes' face appears before her again.

"Okay, so, we're going to let you rest here for a while. There's a change of clothes over on the table—I'm afraid you lost your clothes in the fire."

"My belo—my knife."

"I'm sorry. We found the strap, it's with the clothes, but—I looked everywhere, Alex. It's gone."

Alex squeezes her eyes shut. If she could clench her jaw any tighter, her entire skull would break.

"Anyway. The freight elevator is just a few feet away when you're ready to leave. We switched the electricity back on, so everything's running. Here's my card, and cab fare home—" she feels him slip a tiny envelope into her hand and carefully curl her fingers over it "—and when you're rested and ready to start work, give me a call." The men and women begin closing their notebooks and shoving them into satchels and briefcases.

"Work."

"Yes, Alex." Diogenes lowers his gaze slightly, looking away. He's warning her. "Everyone in Becher District works for the Ministry of Obstetrics, now, and so do you."

"What if I don't want to work for you."

One of the men laughs.

"So you're just going to leave me on the floor, naked and alone."

"We're not babysitters, we have real work to do," one of the younger women snaps.

"Don't worry." The photographer leans over her and takes a final shot, the flash blinding her briefly. "You're never alone in Becher anymore. We'll make sure no one comes near the building. But if we need more observations in the field or need to go over your healing process in greater detail, we know what to do. Contact you, that is."

They're going to kill me, again and again, and again…

"You'll be fine," Diogenes says as he gently squeezes her arm. He leans farther in, and she waits as he opens his mouth to speak. He stares into her eyes—what does he want?

I have faith in you. He mouths the words silently, but her body jolts as hard as if he had screamed them. She feels a single finger press firmly against her upper thigh, right where her gently thrumming knife used to be strapped. And then, with the rest of them, he is gone.

Alex lies on the concrete floor, drifting in and out of sleep. Every five minutes, like clockwork, a little earthquake shakes the building, but after the first twenty or thirty, she drifts right through them. Outside the warehouse, she hears the faint ebb and flow of heavy traffic, as if everything was normal in Becher, as if nothing strange had ever happened here, beyond the normal parameters of strangeness. Pigeons coo from the edges of the skylight, then crack their wings and disappear as hawks dive-bomb them. The shadows shrink, move, lengthen. At some point, Alex makes the decision to sit up. By the time she's in an upright position, back against the wall and legs sprawled out before her, it's night out, but not as she's ever seen it before. A deep unnatural green glow spills down from the skylight. The high walls, she realizes, are blocking out the ambient light of Obsidia. She'll never again see full night, or full day.

It's just Becher down here, just the emerald and aubergine glow of those two massive beams of thaumaturgical power that cross the city from the middle of the spurs, that now creep up the walls, dragging them all behind.

When the weak light of morning appears through the filthy glass panes, Alex finally forces herself to her feet. Her movements are stiff and jerky, and it feels like someone beat the holy fuck out of her. She ignores the tears streaming down her cheeks as she takes her first steps, one hand flat against the rough wall, her silver nails leaving long streaks in the rotting concrete. Another day and night might help, but she's hungry and filthy, and along with the money and business card, Diogenes slipped the key to her apartment into the envelope. It's obviously a copy, which means that the Ministry must have the keys to everything in Becher now, but she doesn't care. It spurs her into action, into slipping the terrible Ministry-issued dress over her head and strapping the worn reminder of her greatest loss in life against her left thigh, into pulling the massive gates to the freight elevator shut even though it hurts so much she starts to laugh, and even though it takes her almost an hour to figure out how to shift the heavy levers that send it down and level enough with the ground floor so she can actually step out without needing a ladder. The main floor is nothing more than another industrial cathedral of colossal pillars of brick and stone, with a modest row of offices lining one side, and a series of loading docks and doors facing opposite. She searches through several of the offices before finding a working phone and crumbling stationery with the name and address of the warehouse.

After she convinces the operator to connect her to a local taxi service, Alex washes up in the dusty locker room. The lights are fat bars of ordinary florescence, and they flicker and buzz like tired yellow jackets when she turns them on. She stands before the cracked sink, water dripping down her face and the face in the mottled mirror. It is the face of a woman who has not lived fifty years, or forty, or even thirty. A new network of jagged black scars and contusions cover her dark skin and all the older shimmering lines; but they'll disappear eventually, and the woman who remains behind will be a woman who has been rebuilt a good quarter-century younger, with brighter teeth, with a touch of mercury flashing at the brown center of her eyes.

"I remember you," Alex says to the face still hiding behind the bruised and swollen trauma. "Hello again." Her fingertips brush the smooth hollow at the throat of her neck. Of course the faked thauma-port is gone. It wasn't a part of her, it was a part of Obsidia, medical and alien trickery rejected in her reshaping. It feels good to see the beating of her heart within that smooth, unobstructed valley of flesh. As her fingers rest in the hollow, Alex notes flashes of white circling her still-mending wrists, little sparks of prismatic light just under the skin. Diamonds, beautiful and unbreakable.

Things are going to be different this time.

Alex makes her way to the main entrance, pushes the large metal door open, and steps outside to a wide cobblestone street lined with identical brick warehouse fronts. The air is dry and there's no horrifying smell to it, which is odd, and the street is quiet, almost sepulcher in feel. The river, she realizes. That constant wet, putrid smell, it's gone. The glare from above is terrible, as always, but already she notes that the great shadow of the new high wall is making a rapid approach from the east—in less than ten minutes, she'll stand in complete shade. Days will be much shorter here, for centuries. And the nights will be longer, but never quite dark enough for those black-clad witches and mages that dart and flow in their mysterious ways through her neighborhood streets. That will change things, make everything a little more interesting and dangerous.

And the wall itself. She cups her hands around her eyes and stares at it. It glistens slightly, from the constant trickling of the remains of the Becher running down its walls. Lubricant, Alex thinks with a shudder, for the ease of

Becher's glorious ascent as the one who comes before whatever it's pulling up from the depths of the planet's womb. She wonders how many will try to scale the wall in an attempt to escape. She wonders how many will try to burrow below, to see what they can see. She wonders which one of those groups she'll join, or if she'll find another, entirely different purpose and way.

A horn honks—she turns to see a rusting red taxi slowing as it makes its way to her. She's going home. For the first time in she can't remember how long, Alex feels a kind of lightness in her heart. Is this happiness? She doesn't dare say yes.

"You know where we're going, right?" she asks as she opens the door and slides into the back seat.

"Yes, ma'am, I got the address from dispatch—146 Bernd Street, Powerhouse Parish." The cabbie starts off down the street. "That's where all the big-ass factories and machines are, right? Some serious fucking dark magic going on there, some real black shit."

"You are correct."

"You're a long way from home this morning. Or, today, this afternoon, I really don't know what the fuck to call it anymore."

"Yeah. I really am." Alex rolls down the window and lets the air stream over her face. It's far cooler than yesterday, there's almost a bite to the air. Relocating over half a mile below the surface has some benefits, apparently.

"You look like you had a rough night."

"I most certainly did."

"What did you do? If you don't mind my asking. Orgy?"

"I tortured and killed a couple of people, then I quit my job and killed and helped throw a few of my coworkers into the engines of those big machines that came to life and brought us down here; and then I died and brought myself back to life. Twice."

"Ha. Okay. Rough couple of nights. Was it worth it?"

Alex stares outside. They're on Calatrava Boulevard now, heading back into the heart of Becher, and she's shocked to see how many people there are, how many remained behind. Cars and trolleys and horse-drawn wagons, clogged traffic of all shapes and sorts, horns blaring and pedestrians running or flying across the streets, screaming obscenities and spells. The clang of church bells and cry of police sirens. The roar of a city in full gear, clamped on the body of some great and enigmatic god as it forces its way out of the womb of the earth to be born.

"I don't know. You tell me."

The cabbie shrugs. "As long as I have passengers, I'm fine with it. I mean, I'm sure things are gonna change, but people still need to get places, so I'm good."

"Okay, then. It was worth it."

"Bet you'll never do it again, though, right?"

Alex doesn't respond. She's staring down at the side of her left leg, still almost black with bruises and dried blood. Peeking out of the empty sheath is a tiny square of paper, bright pink. She plucks it out, and peels it open. One of Quartus's Post-It notes. Neat block letters, just like yesterday.

THE FINAL DELIVERY
MUST NOT BE COMPLETED
YOU ARE THE WEAPON
WE WILL USE AGAIN
~WE HAVE FAITH IN YOU~

"I said, I bet you'll never do that again, right?"

Alex flops back against the leather seat, and stares at the back of the cabbie's fat, oily head as she raises her hands in front of her face. Her silver fingernails begin, ever so faintly, to vibrate and thrum. All the beloved bones in her body follow suit; and the avenue turns silver like the stars.

"Oh, I wouldn't bet on that."

ABOUT THE AUTHOR

Livia Llewellyn is a writer of dark fantasy, horror, and erotica, whose short fiction has appeared in over forty anthologies and magazines and has been reprinted in multiple best-of anthologies, including Ellen Datlow's *The Best Horror of the Year* series, *Year's Best Weird Fiction*, and *The Mammoth Book of Best Erotica*. Her first collection, *Engines of Desire: Tales of Love & Other Horrors* (2011, Lethe Press), received two Shirley Jackson Award nominations for Best Collection, and for Best Novelette (for "Omphalos"). Her story "Furnace" received a 2013 Shirley Jackson Award nomination for Best Short Story. Her second collection, *Furnace* (2016, Word Horde Press), received a 2016 Shirley Jackson Award nomination for Best Collection. You can find her online at liviallewellyn.com, and on Instagram and Twitter.

ACKNOWLEDGEMENTS

Many thanks to Brian Keene for inviting me and authors Rachel Deering, Chesya Burke, and Amber Fallon to publish our novellas in his Maelstrom imprint anthology, despite the protestation of a few horror fans who seemed convinced that publishing a bunch of damn females could only bring about the downfall of the genre (for better or for worse, it did not). Thanks also to Alessandro Manzetti for giving my novella a second life, to George Cotronis for the spectacular cover art, and to Jodi Renée Lester for her meticulous edits. And as always, thanks to my writing work husband Robert Levy, for his endless love and support.

FORTHCOMING BOOKS

THE WISH MECHANICS
by Daniel Braum
Collection – **Paperback and eBook Edition**
June 2017

THE BEAUTY OF DEATH 2 – DEATH BY WATER
Anthology – **Paperback and eBook Edition**
Edited by Alessandro Manzetti and Jodi Renée Lester
October 2017

AVAILABLE BOOKS

SELECTED STORIES
by Nate Southard
Collection – **Paperback and eBook Edition**
April 2017

THE CARP-FACED BOY AND OTHER TALES
by Thersa Matsuura
Collection – **Paperback and eBook Edition**
February 2017

ALL-AMERICAN HORROR OF THE 21ST CENTURY
Edited by MortCastle
Anthology – **Paperback and eBook Edition**
November 2016

BENEATH THE NIGHT
by Greg F. Gifune
Novel & Novella – **Paperback Edition**
October 2016

THE BEAUTY OF DEATH
Edited by Alessandro Manzetti
Anthology – **eBook Edition**
July 2016

DOCTOR BRITE
by Poppy Z. Brite
Collection – **eBook Edition**
January 2017

WHAT WE FOUND IN THE WOODS
by Shane McKenzie
Collection – **eBook Edition**
September 2016

USED STORIES
by Poppy Z. Brite
Collection – **eBook Edition**
June 2016

THE HORROR SHOW
by Poppy Z. Brite
Collection – **eBook Edition**
August 2016

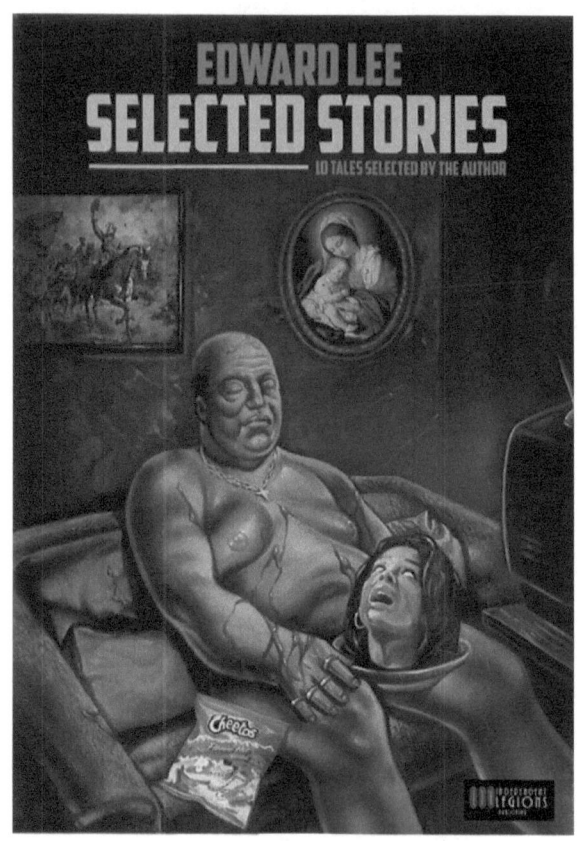

SELECTED STORIES
by Edward Lee
Collection – **eBook Edition**
July 2016

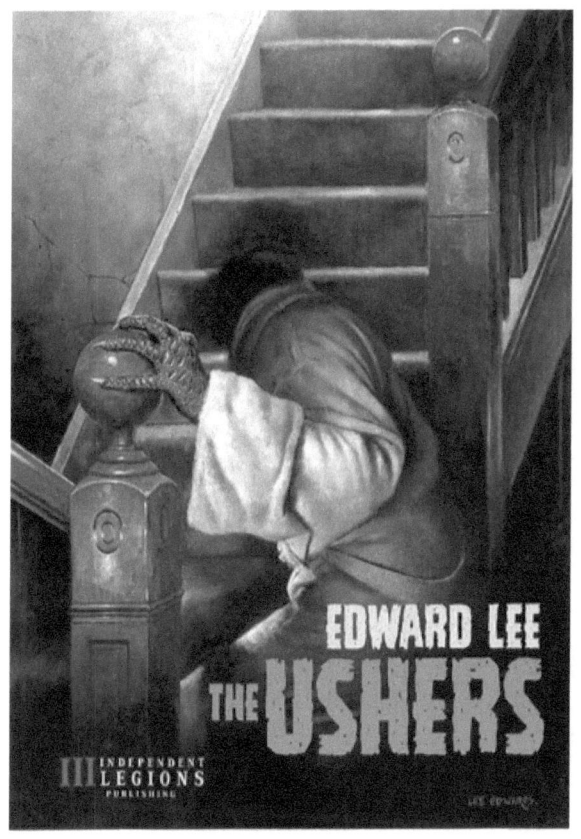

THE USHERS
by Edward Lee
Collection – **eBook Edition**
May 2016

THE CRYSTAL EMPIRE
by Poppy Z. Brite
Novella – **eBook Edition**
May 2016

SELECTED STORIES
by Poppy Z. Brite
Collection – **eBook Edition**
February 2016

THE HITCHHIKING EFFECT
by Gene O'Neill
Collection – **eBook Edition**
February 2016

SONGS FOR THE LOST
by Alexander Zelenyj
Collection – **eBook Edition**
April 201

INDEPENDENT LEGIONS PUBLISHING
by Alessandro Manzetti
Via Castelbianco, 8 - 00168 Roma (Italy)

www.independentlegions.com
www.facebook.com/independentlegions

Books in Italian:
www.independentlegions.com/pubblicazioni.html